# FOR ALL
# TIME

## Other Books by Caroline B. Cooney

# FOR ALL
# TIME

*Caroline B. Cooney*

DELACORTE PRESS

Published by
Delacorte Press
an imprint of
Random House Children's Books
a division of Random House, Inc.
1540 Broadway
New York, New York 10036

Visit us on the Web! www.randomhouse.com/teens
Educators and librarians, for a variety of teaching tools, visit us at
www.randomhouse.com/teachers

Library of Congress Catalonging-in-Publication Data

Cooney, Caroline B.
  For all time / Caroline B. Cooney.
    p. cm.
  Sequel to: Prisoner of time.
  Summary: Annie, a teenager in 1999, tries to travel back in time to join her lost love Strat in Egypt in 1899, but instead she ends up in ancient Egypt and in great danger.
  ISBN 0-385-32773-0 (trade) — ISBN 0-385-90019-8 (lib. bdg.)
  1. Egypt—Civilization—To 332 B.C.—Juvenile fiction.
[1. Egypt—Civilization—To 332 B.C.—Fiction.   2. Time travel—Fiction.]   I. Title.
  PZ7.C7834 Fo 2001
  [Fic]—dc21
                            2001017216

The text of this book is set in 13-point Granjon.
Book design by Susan Clark Dominguez

Manufactured in the United States of America
October 2001
BVG   10 9 8 7 6 5 4 3 2 1

*For my granddaughter*
*Elizabeth Anne*

# I

*Time to Fight*

# ANNIE: 1999

When her parents finally got married again and left for their honeymoon, nobody was happier than Annie Lockwood.

She now had four days—precisely ninety-six hours—in which she would be unsupervised. Annie had convinced her parents that while they were gone, she would be responsible, trustworthy and dependable.

None of this was true. Every single promise to her mother and father she had no intention of keeping.

She was alone at last. The wedding guests were gone and her parents en route to Florida. Her brother was on a bus with his team, headed to basketball camp. The house was utterly quiet. Annie stood in the center of her bedroom, unaware of the clutter around her, and gathered her courage.

Opening her top desk drawer, Annie removed a small envelope and shook it until a scrap of newspaper fell out. It landed between a mug of pencils and a stack of CDs.

**EGYPTIAN ART IN THE AGE OF THE PYRAMIDS**
**September 16, 1999—January 9, 2000**

1

## Metropolitan Museum of Art
## New York, New York

Annie despised museums. Whenever there was a class trip to a museum, she tried to be sick and stay home for the day. If this failed, she slouched in the teacher's wake, wishing she could get pushed around in a wheelchair, because nothing was more tiring than standing in front of a painting.

But today was different. In a few hours, Annie would be standing in front of a photograph which had merited one brief mention in the newspaper article about the special exhibition. Taken one hundred years ago, this portrait showed every member of the original archaeology expedition.

And would the person she cared about most, the person she had known one hundred years ago, be in that photograph? How vividly Annie remembered Strat's moppy hair and broad shoulders, his casual grin and easy slouch. Every time she touched the newsprint, she felt Strat through the ink.

Strat was in Egypt, waiting for her.

She could feel him. She would cross Time and be with him again.

Four days lay ahead of her. Surely Time understood the urgency and would bring her to Strat.

Annie unzipped her bridesmaid dress. It was a fashion disaster in emergency room green, which indeed made Annie look as if she needed to be hospitalized. Why had Mom's college roommate agreed to put this dress on her body twenty years ago, when she was maid of honor? Why had this roommate saved the dress, so that Annie would have to wear it in public?

But in the end, wearing such a dress was a small sacrifice to celebrate that her mother and father were not getting divorced after all.

Dad's hobby for the last few years had been another woman. Annie and her brother hadn't expected their parents to have another anniversary, let alone another wedding. But not only did Mom and Dad seem truly back together, Mom had talked Dad into getting married a second time for their twentieth anniversary.

When Mom came down the aisle, as lovely as ever in her original white satin wedding gown, even Annie's cynical brother, Tod, was dabbing at tears. Annie chose to believe that Dad repeated his vows—broken once—with every intention of keeping them this time around.

The word *time* had swirled throughout every conversation of the second wedding day.

My parents loved and lost, thought Annie. Today, they swore to love again. I loved and lost. Today, I, too, will have a second chance.

She let the ghastly dress fall onto the carpet and stepped out of it. Annie was fond of floors, which were the best storage space. She kicked off her dyed-to-match satin shoes, peeled away her stockings and stood barefoot and happy in front of her closet. She had even bought clothing from an adventure catalog to wear for this museum trip.

She put on the long swirling skirt of khaki twill; the

3

full-sleeved silky white blouse; the jacket with bright buttons and many pockets. She tied a scarlet scarf loosely at her throat and pulled on footgear that was half army boot, half sneaker, and fully cool.

In the full-length mirror, with her pale complexion and sleek dark hair falling to her waist, she had a dated look, like a young schoolmarm from another time.

She drew some deep breaths, preparing herself, trying to still her racing heart and hopes. She had never gone into New York City alone. The kick of the city was going with friends. But if Annie was right about this, she would meet the friend she cared about most in the museum. He would be in the photograph, waiting.

She would climb through.

# STRAT: 1899

S trat was riding a camel.

He had expected a camel to be like a horse. He would become friends with his camel, which would trot to meet him in the morning and nuzzle him affectionately.

Camels, however, despised Strat. They spat and growled, they gave him dirty looks, they tried to bite and they never stopped making nasty noises.

Strat had had stepmothers like this camel.

His father had had two activities in life: money and marriage. Father had been extremely good at money, but not good at wives. But then, money was worth holding on to and wives were not. For this and other reasons, Strat hoped never to speak to, write to, or be in the same room with, his father again.

But once he mounted the camel (sitting on something more like a table than a saddle, with pillows and backrest, a carpet and a sunshade), the camel forgot Strat was there, as indeed Strat hoped Father had forgotten about him. Riding a camel was like sitting in a rocking chair that happened to progress toward the horizon. Strat could bring a picnic or a book, write a letter or take a nap.

Today, however, he was bringing two dead bodies into Cairo.

The bodies were wrapped in a canvas tent flap. The Egyptian servants had first draped the bodies over a donkey's back, but Egyptian donkeys were very small, so the bodies hung with their heads dangling in the dust on one side and their feet on the other. The loss of dignity was great. Strat had to bring them up onto the camel with him.

It was not as awful as he would have expected to have two dead bodies in his lap. In Egypt, who could fail to think of death? The land itself was death, blazing murderous desert encircling stone cities of the dead, occupied now by whole cities of archaeologists. Strat's archaelogist, Dr. Lightner, searched for death. It was Dr. Lightner's great hope to find a mummy in a royal tomb, untouched by Time or robbers.

Even Strat's camera was death. It recorded on paper what had existed a moment ago but would never exist in the same way again.

Strat had been dreaming of death. In the dream, he was buried alive. When a shaft leading to a long-lost tomb was opened, he, Strat, tumbled in and was forgotten, to be smothered by shovelsful of sand and bucketsful of stone as the shaft was filled in. The dream was so vivid that Strat would wake up with his fingers scrabbling at the low tent ceiling, trying to claw through canvas to get air.

He wondered what the two French campers had been dreaming of when they rolled over in their sleep.

The Egyptians had refused to deal with the bodies. The Pyramid, they said, was fine to climb by day, but by night, it belonged to the ghosts of the past. Persons on the Pyramid at night should expect to be accosted by the spirits of those who had gone before.

How Dr. Lightner scoffed. "You and I, of course," he said to Strat, as they packed the bodies, "have no such superstitious beliefs."

Dr. Lightner was incorrect. *Superstitious* meant believing in things inconsistent with the known laws of science. Strat had witnessed something inconsistent with the known laws of science. Father had imprisoned Strat in a lunatic asylum because of what Strat claimed. So Strat could not quite so easily dismiss the idea of ghosts from the past.

He had volunteered to go to the French embassy in Cairo because he could not bear to think of the families who would not know what had happened to their boys. Strat knew what it was like never to have answers about the fate of somebody you loved.

Everybody was delighted not to have to think of the dead tourists again and they were quite cheery as they waved good-bye to Strat.

Egypt was crammed with tourists. Boats overflowed with archaeologists; camels were top-heavy with dreamers; donkeys were laden with watercolor artists. Strat made all his spending money by taking photographs of elderly British maiden ladies and spry old Italian men, of sparkly uniformed British soldiers en route to conquer the Sudan and pipe-smoking German scholars who argued with Dr. Lightner's conclusions.

Tourists paid well, and the more money he made, the more he could send to Katie. Not that it was money Katie needed. In her letters, she assured Strat that she was proud of him and that was enough, he need send no dollars.

It was not enough, and Strat knew this utterly.

Katie wanted love, but Strat had given away the love he possessed. He had given love to his family, and in return, had been destroyed by his own father. He had given love to Harriett, and she had died. He had given love to Annie, and she was lost to another world.

Strat was still a nice person who knew his duty. But his heart was desiccated, like the hearts of mummies in tombs: a hard dry thing, without hope. And now he lurched on a camel with dead men whose hopes had ended.

Oh, Annie! he thought, staring at the burned gold of desert sand. Will I ever see you again?

Time was flying by. It was November of 1899. In six short weeks, Time would hurtle around a huge and magnificent corner, becoming another century.

*Nineteen hundred.*

If Strat did not cross Time now, he never would.

And so Strat decided that he, too, would spend the night on top of the Pyramid, in the hope that the Egyptians were correct and he would meet the spirits of those who had gone before.

He approached the French embassy in the belief that he had everything under control. He even spoke a little French, which was good, because Frenchmen felt that the English language—especially spoken with an American accent—was a poor way to communicate.

But after the spoken formalities were over, there were paper formalities. Forms to be filled out. Signatures.

Strat had not expected to need his name.

Everybody at the dig called him Strat and never asked for more. He was not one of the impressive young men, college boys from Yale or Princeton who were playing at archaeology for a few months before joining their fathers' law firms in Boston. He was merely the camera boy, practically a servant.

He should have come up with a false name long before, but he had been too dumb. He had thought thousands of miles would protect him from the name Hiram Stratton. Strat pasted a fake smile on his face and scribbled. "Archibald Lightner."

The French turned cold. He was no longer forgiven for being American. "You will sign your own name," they said sharply, "not your employer's."

"I'm not in charge," he protested.

They whipped out a fresh form. "You brought the bodies. You sign."

He could have chosen any name. John Strat. Strat Johnson. But he panicked and scribbled a meaningless squash of letters. He found himself with a cold and severe Frenchman.

Why was he reluctant to state his real name? the

attaché demanded. What made him volunteer to dispose of the bodies? Where had Strat been, at midnight, when the two boys supposedly rolled over and fell to their deaths?

The attaché pulled the ends of his mustache into thin cords, revealing thin lips tightened in suspicion. "How did these boys die?" asked the officer. "Did you push them?"

# ANNIE: 1999

Annie climbed the Grand Staircase of the Metropolitan Museum, silently thanking every benefactor whose name was recorded on the marble panels on either side of her. New York would be less grand without this museum, and these were the men and women who had provided it.

Then she forgot everything except the special exhibition.

It was divided among rooms whose gray carpet went right up the walls, giving both exhibition and visitors a padded permanent look, as though they would be here forever, enclosed in cloudy gray. She was bumped by two very old ladies with museum headsets perched in their white curls. A girl in frayed black sweats sat cross-legged on the floor, sketching a statue whose eyes had been ripped out in antiquity. A middle-aged man read the translation of an ancient papyrus, while a tiny delicate woman studied a trinket box carved from hippopotamus ivory.

There were a number of photographs. Each one had a caption. LIGHTNER EXPEDITION. 1899.

The first one Annie studied was not framed, just tacked to splintered wood. It was black and white, yet full of glare and heat. It showed a woman caught in a whip of sand and dust, arm raised against her face so she could breathe, her long skirt billowing, and beyond her, the rising side of a vast pyramid.

Who was the woman? The placard did not say.

Maybe it's me, thought Annie Lockwood.

The contents of the next room had come from the tomb of a queen named Hetepheres, mother of King Khufu, who built the Great Pyramid.

The tomb of Hetepheres had been found entirely by accident when a cameraman employed by the archaeologists got clumsy. His heavy wooden tripod fell over, striking a patch of plaster that had hitherto concealed the entrance to the shaft.

The placard did not give the name of the cameraman.

Was it Strat?

If she could touch the photo, she'd know. She'd feel Strat through that paper. Or she wouldn't.

A museum guard, finely tuned to be aware of all ready-to-touch visitors, gave Annie the heavy-lidded look of authority.

She stumbled on.

In the third room was a small gold statue of Sekhmet, goddess of revenge, on a pedestal behind glass. And there, at eye level on the carpeted wall, was the photograph described in the newspaper article: every member of the dig that had uncovered the tomb of Hetepheres.

Museum visitors were standing in front of it and

blocking Annie's view. She peered around shoulders and between the straps of handbags.

The picture was large, with the quiet hazy look of early photographs. A dozen people had posed in two rows, shadowed by the brims of hats they had worn a hundred years ago to protect themselves from the Egyptian sun. They seemed to have been mummified as they waited for the picture to be taken.

Slowly the exhibition visitors rotated on. One boy was still half in Annie's way, but she couldn't wait any longer, even though she wanted to be alone with her photograph. She shouldered the boy away and carefully examined each tiny black-and-white face. This had to be her shaft through Time.

But Strat was not in the photograph.

Annie was just a silly girl in silly clothing, wearing her silly hopes. "Oh, Strat!" she said, heart bursting with grief.

The boy who was also still looking at the photograph said, "Yes?"

# CAMILLA: 1899

Six months after the murder of her father, Camilla Mateusz decided to become a man, because men were paid more. She had read once that a Confederate girl pretended to be a soldier throughout the entire War Between the States and never got caught. So why couldn't Camilla be a man during the twelve working hours of the day—and never get caught?

Camilla possessed an advantage in such a masquerade. She towered over all ladies and most men.

A lady must be delicate, with white throat and narrow ankles. Not that anybody believed a Polish girl was within reach of being a lady, but Camilla Mateusz had an additional affliction. She was six feet tall in a generation where most girls were hardly more than five. When she was sitting, people thought her attractive, and praised the thick blond braids, rosy cheeks and blue eyes.

Eventually, however, Camilla had to stand up. Mill hand or shopkeeper, priest or policeman—everybody who saw Camilla unfold burst out laughing. Who would ever marry her?

Only once had her height been useful, in the wonderful new game called basketball. How grand to feel the joy men had always felt: throwing a ball.

Of course, girls did not play the same game as boys. Girls, for example, could not dribble, which was a skill far beyond their capacities. The court was only half as large, and in long skirts, girls did not move quickly. Last season, however, the girls had actually been permitted to play against another school's team. Oh, not without arguments. The community was outraged by this attack against feminine behavior. It was clear where this kind of thing would lead. Lovely sweet girls would be ruined.

They pointed to Camilla as proof, how unwomanly she was, with her attention to the ball and her desire to win.

Well, Camilla had lost the joy of basketball. She had lost her chance to win a high school diploma as well. But she had not lost her father's courage. He had crossed a terrible ocean, worked hard at a terrible job and died a terrible death. He had done this for his family and she could not do less.

What to do about the waist-length yellow hair of which she was so proud?

Since men wore caps or hats in the street, as a man, she could cover her hair to an extent, but caps were removed indoors. Camilla would have to have short hair. And so she gave herself a ragged haircut, put on Papa's clothing and Papa's cap. Low on her cheeks she rubbed a little soot from the kerosene lamp. Then she put on Papa's old reading glasses, smudging them a bit in hope of lessening the blue of her eyes.

Oh, Papa! He had had his heart set on seeing his

children finish school. *They* would not spend their lives in a mine or mill. *They* would go to an office, have clean jobs and wear white shirts with white collars.

The Mateusz family had but one photograph on their walls. It was large and quiet in its heavy brown frame. Mama was seated, Papa standing behind her, his hand resting on her shoulder. Mama wore the dress she had been married in and Papa his only suit—the one in which he had lately been buried. Seven children stood around them, solemn and proud to be in a portrait. Since then, the three oldest had had to drop out of school to work in the mills—or rather, the remaining mill; the one Mr. Hiram Stratton had *not* burned down; the one in which her father had *not* died.

This morning Mama had had no food to put in the lunch pails. Irena and Magdalena, Antony and Marya did not cry. They just looked a little more pinched as they set out for school. Stefan, age thirteen, shrugged and walked out to endure his twelve-hour day. But Jerzy paused for a moment, running his fingers over the pile of his abandoned schoolbooks, still stacked on the shelf by the door. He made a fist, hit the wall, apologized to his mother and went to the factory. Jerzy was fourteen.

Mr. Hiram Stratton, Sr., the man whose wealth and needs dictated all that happened in this city, had broken a strike by the simple expedient of burning down the factory. He had not checked to see if the factory was empty. He ordered his thugs to torch it, and they did. Michael Mateusz had been there. He had not gotten out.

Hiram Stratton was not accused of arson. He was not accused of murder. In fact, he was named the next police commissioner.

So Camilla left a note for her mother. "I've gone to get a good job. I will send money so the boys can return to school. Do not worry about me. I am strong."

Newspaper advertisements contained four possible jobs. The first three interviews went badly. She blushed when she pretended to be Cameron Matthews instead of Camilla Mateusz. She lowered her eyes demurely, forgetting to stare man to man. She did not remember to stride or swing her arms. Furthermore, she went in the morning, while sunlight streamed into each office. Nobody guessed that this very tall person could be a girl, but they were puzzled and uncertain and did not want to hire her.

The fourth interview was late in the afternoon. Camilla found herself at an office that did not yet have electric lights, and the single lamp in the little room scarcely illuminated the papers on the desk, never mind the stranger in the door. She paused for courage, reading the sign.

DUFFIE DETECTIVE AGENCY.
WE FOLLOW YOUR SPOUSE.
WE FIND YOUR MONEY.

Camilla's heart sank.
She could not be party to the sort of things that led to

divorce! Aside from the fact that the Church would disapprove, she might lose faith in the human race.

Although, given what Hiram Stratton had done, what faith had she in the human race anyway?

She raised her hand to cross herself, and keep away the evil of such practices as arson and divorce, when she was greeted by the man who must be Mr. Duffie. Just in time, Camilla remembered that her pretend self, Cameron Matthews, was probably not a good Catholic.

But Mr. Duffie thought she meant to shake hands, so he got halfway up from his desk, extending his hand over the wide wooden top. Luckily she had been doing this all day and knew to grip hard.

His black pomaded hair glistened on his head. He might, or might not, have brushed his teeth the week before. He handed her a form to fill out.

*Cameron Matthews,* she wrote, in big strong script.

*High school diploma,* she added, instead of *Eighth-grade graduate.*

Mr. Duffie held her paperwork close to the lamp and scanned the page quickly. "Matthews," he said approvingly. "A good English name. You don't know how many Poles and Czechs come in here, expecting to be hired, as if they were regular people."

Camilla spat into the tobacco stand to demonstrate her disgust at the current situation in America. This was a hard part of being a man. Why did men always have spit in their mouths? She certainly never had any spare spit in her mouth.

Mr. Duffie leaned back in a wooden swivel chair and

chewed the tip of a pipe. "What I need, Mr. Matthews," said Duffie, "is a man willing to masquerade as a woman. I know, I know. A shameful thing to ask. I have had men vomit at the suggestion of imitating a female. But in this line of work, there are situations into which a man cannot go. A female, however, could do so."

That would be interesting, thought Camilla. I'd be a woman pretending to be a man pretending to be a woman. "Why then," she asked, in her new deep voice, "do you not simply hire a female?"

Mr. Duffie laughed out loud. "Nobody would trust the evidence of a female. Who would hire my agency if it became known that I used female operatives? No, I need a man to disguise himself."

"You ask a great deal," said Camilla, accepting the offer of chewing tobacco.

"I pay a great deal, Mr. Matthews," said Mr. Duffie, writing the amount on a piece of paper and shoving it toward her.

Camilla nearly swallowed her tobacco. He told the truth. He paid a great deal. If she lived frugally, not only could Jerzy and Stefan return to school, lunch pails would be full! Mama could pay somebody else to do the laundry!

Camilla trembled with the desire to have all that money, but suppressed her shiver as unmanly.

"Well, Matthews?" demanded Duffie.

"I shall undertake the task, humiliating though it will be to act like a woman. You will call me Cameron as a man, and Camilla as a woman. You will give me an advance against my salary so that I may purchase female garments. Is this Camilla Matthews to be rich? Or some poor shopwoman? Is she to read and write? Should she talk with an accent? Describe her to me."

The detective was impressed. "You are going to be excellent, Mr. Matthews," he said. "Or should I say, Miss Matthews? You and I will make a great team."

And so it began.

The loneliest, strangest life Camilla could imagine. There could be no friends or family. There could not even be the Church. Tell a priest the sins she was daily committing? The sinful people she followed and watched? The sinful people from whom she accepted pay?

She lived in a boardinghouse, never going home, lest her family grasp the shameful, scandalous decision she had made. Were Jerzy and Stefan ever to understand the life their sister was leading, they would refuse her money, quit school again and go back to the mills. So Camilla mailed the money to her mother.

The boardinghouse was for men only, of course. Boardinghouses did not mix the sexes. She shared a bathroom with the other five boarders. This was an extraordinary difficulty. But she managed in part because the other five cared nothing for cleanliness.

At night, safe under rough sheets, Cameron-Camilla Matthews could be Camilla Mateusz again. She would smother her pain against the pillow, yearning to be back in school, studying history, increasing her math skills and translating her Latin.

But she was the man of the family now. When a man had a family to support, he must forget himself and his plans.

And so the months dragged on. Once, dressed as Cameron Matthews, she strolled past the grammar school to feast her eyes on Irena and Magdalena, Antony and Marya. The girls wore new dresses! Their cheeks were pink with good health. Antony had his own baseball bat.

Sitting on the stoop of a tenement, pretending to fix her bootlaces, Camilla saw Jerzy dash out of the adjacent high school, joyfully taking the steps two at a time, running across the paved playground to greet the little ones. She heard him laugh.

And so she went on with her masquerade. But she did not laugh.

At least she could let her hair grow out. When she had to be Cameron Matthews, she wore a cap, pinning her hair safely beneath it. But when she was Camilla, she could brush her hair and admire how yellow it was, buy a ribbon and try on hats.

She visited Duffie only at dusk, when the man was exhausted, ready to go to his own boardinghouse for dinner, wishing to spend as little time with her as possible. She had already ascertained that his eyesight was poor and his spectacles unhelpful. He saw only the tall gawky frame of Cameron Matthews, and unless she made a large blunder, Duffie would never realize the secret of her gender.

"Today, Mr. Matthews," said Duffie, "I have for you

an extraordinary assignment. You will have heard of the great gentleman, Hiram Stratton, Sr.—the railroad millionaire."

Camilla was almost sick with an evil hope. Perhaps Stratton's current wife was trying to divorce him. Perhaps Camilla was to have a chance to ruin the man. "I believe Hiram Stratton also owned a factory in the city at one time," said Camilla.

"Yes, it burned down. We're not involved with that. We're after the son. Hiram Stratton, Jr."

Camilla had not known there was a son. How dare Hiram Stratton, Sr., enjoy a son, while Michael Mateusz would never see his sons grow up?

"The son ran away," said Mr. Duffie. "It's a very sad story. He had to be punished for a serious dereliction of duty to his father. He was kept in a private asylum so that he might come to his senses. However, the boy fled from his captivity. Not only did he attack a doctor, but he kidnapped two fellow patients! He did it not for ransom, but for disguise, so that he might look like a family man. I cannot imagine how he pulled it off."

Disguise was overrated. If Camilla could trick the world, so could a sneaky sly son of a Stratton.

"How the great man dreams of a joyful reunion with his long-lost son," said Duffie.

Great man, indeed. Why was it that any man of wealth was great, no matter how he acquired his money or what he did with it? Camilla wanted to know.

"I was honored when the great man chose me to find the boy. I have been working on this, Mr. Matthews, and at last, have an avenue to follow. Stratton junior took his two victims to Spain, where he abandoned them. I am sending you to Spain to interview the female and obtain Junior's current address."

Spain! thought Camilla. Spain of bullfighters and flamenco dancers? Spain of a thousand castles? "Tell me about the kidnap victims," she said.

"Shocking," replied Duffie. "One was a young man with so small a brain he never learned how to talk; the other, a woman with a hideously deformed body. Naturally their parents put them away. We do not have the female's full name, since her family, of course, did not want the shame of admitting her existence. She wasn't identified by a last name even in the asylum records. But her first name is Katie. You will find her involved with some sort of hospital. St. Rafael. She seems to be a nurse now, rather than a patient."

Insane asylums were often kind enough to take in defectives, and perhaps the creature really had learned nursing skills. Camilla's heart broke for such a girl. What pain must she have met at the hands of Hiram Stratton, Jr.?

"But how will Mr. Stratton prevent a trial of young Stratton for the kidnappings?" asked Camilla. "Surely the parents of the two innocent victims will require justice."

"It is my understanding," said Duffie, "that the parents find it amusing. After all, they need no longer pay for care. No, do not concern yourself with them. As for a trial, naturally Mr. Stratton has paid everybody off. Such a low-class scandal must not be made public. No, we wish to accomplish the joyful reunion of father and son."

I cannot bring joy to a Stratton! thought Camilla.

Mr. Duffie pared his nails. He did this when he was lying. "For this task," he said casually, "you will be Camilla Matthews. You will offer comfort, real or false, whatever works. Promise the girl anything in order to get young Stratton's location. Mr. Stratton is providing a large expense account and you will spend whatever is necessary. You will cable me, of course, with every development."

Camilla was no saint, to walk away from assignments that paid well. And it might be that in Spain, she could arrange things to her own satisfaction: Destroy the father and ruin the son.

Camilla's heart raced in the ugly hot emotion of revenge. Oh, to have more power than Hiram Stratton! To shove in his face what he had shoved in hers! "I will go to Spain. I will need a large advance." She named an outrageous figure.

Duffie sputtered and refused.

She unfolded, her six feet casting a threatening shadow over his desk. "I could inform Mr. Stratton that you are already cutting corners."

They glared at each other and Duffie broke first. "Matthews, you are exactly right for this job. You shall have what you ask."

How wonderful were the long voyage and the days of female company. How she cherished being once more part of the conversations and laughter and kindness of women. What a delight to discuss hair and fashion, children and church.

And yet . . . being a woman again was not altogether satisfactory.

Camilla could no longer read a newspaper. She could no longer hold an opinion, nor be interested in sports and politics. As a man, she had commanded respect. As a woman, she was simply a creature too tall to be a dance partner.

Throughout the voyage, she studied Spanish, memorizing useful sentences, but once she arrived, as soon as she mentioned the name of the hospital—St. Rafael—every Spaniard melted away, saying nothing.

When, after several days, Camilla stumbled on St. Rafael, she knew why Mr. Stratton could get nobody else to interview Katie and why he did not go himself. She knew why Duffie had lied, pretending he was not aware of Katie's situation.

It was a leper hospital.

Dreaded since the beginning of time, lepers were shunned for good reason. Before leprosy killed the patient, it first killed the nose and lips and fingers and feet, which rotted and fell off. The image of Katie nauseated Camilla: deformed to start with—now a leper. She could not help imagining herself a leper. To interview Katie, not only must Camilla expose herself to this evil disease, she must lie to the nuns who ran St. Rafael.

For many hours, the twin desires for money and revenge were not enough to make her approach the lepers. At last, however, Camilla summoned her courage. "I am here," she said to the nun who kept the gate, "in hope of visiting your nurse Katie. I have been sent by Devonny Stratton, who seeks news of her dear brother, Strat." Camilla knew nothing of Devonny Stratton, except that the debutante had recently married a titled Englishman and was therefore also out of the country and her father's clutches. "Devonny prays that in spite of the suffering inflicted upon her, Katie will assist in this endeavor."

The nun said nothing.

Camilla remembered her instructions. Promise anything, whether you plan to do it or not. "Miss Stratton wishes to bring Katie home to America, and provide her with the means to live comfortably. Or should she prefer to stay here, to make a major donation to this very hospital."

Nobody was going to give Katie a penny and as for taking her out of the leper hospital, allowing the dreaded infection into society—absurd. Not for any number of dollars.

The nun inclined her head, and rustled away to deliver the message. There was a long wait, during which Camilla's courage dwindled. She fiddled with the lacy white cotton gloves that were part of her everyday clothing. Could mere gloves protect her from leprosy?

The nun returned. Katie would welcome Miss Matthews in her room.

Camilla was aghast. Go *inside*?

"Be not afraid," said the nun gently, in English, as if accustomed to fearful American girls. "It takes years of exposure to acquire leprosy. An hour will not put you at risk. You will find Katie a delight, and glad to speak with a friend of Devonny Stratton. Follow me."

Not at risk? Camilla thought. Of course I'm at risk! From time immemorial, people have known better than to get within rock-throwing distance of a leper.

She reminded herself of the money she would be paid. I'll stay only a minute, she promised herself. When I leave, I'll buy borax and scrub myself for hours.

Katie was heavily garbed in white, even more veiled than the nun. Only her eyes and hands were exposed. Katie offered a hand to be shaken. Camilla had no choice, but she would burn the glove later.

"I am not diseased, Miss Matthews," said Katie gently. "I wear this veil so you will not see my deformities. My mother and father gave me to an asylum for storage, just as lepers are stored here. A decent and good person saved me from that asylum. Here indeed I try to be an equally good and decent person to others."

"That's why I've come," said Camilla. "Devonny is so very very worried about her beloved brother. She has had no news. She fears for his fate, now that he has become a kidnapper."

Katie laughed behind the veil. "I was not kidnapped. I was saved from a life of torment in a house of cruelty. In decency and in honor Strat left behind that which he loved and brought me here."

Women! thought Camilla. How we fall for anything a man says. "Would you tell me what young Mr. Stratton did that could be called honorable? Because I must admit to you that others disagree."

When Katie turned and went to sit on a small stool, a table set for tea was revealed: two cups, sugar and lemons. Drink tea poured by the hand of a leper? Camilla gagged.

"Strat and I crossed the ocean together, pretending to be brother and sister," explained Katie. "When we arrived penniless in Spain, we stayed at a convent and pretended to be on a pilgrimage. I was awestruck by the work of the nuns and I embraced their holy lives. Strat chose adventure and sailed on."

That was one way to look at it. Another was that Junior, having dragged her across the ocean, now dropped her off to die among the lepers.

"And the second person young Mr. Stratton so generously brought along?" said Camilla.

"Poor Douglass was born with very little brain," said Katie. "His parents, like mine, stored him in the asylum. Strat brought both of us to safety. I have Douglass with me here. He is happy. All is well, Miss Matthews."

All is well? Such sainthood made Camilla want to race out into the streets and do something wicked.

"And young Mr. Stratton?" she said carefully. "Is *he* safe? Is *he* happy? His dear sister misses him painfully and hopes for communication."

From a tin box on a rickety wooden table by her narrow bed, Katie removed a packet of letters. She cradled them in her two hands like a bouquet, drinking in their scent.

Camilla tried to see the return address on the envelopes.

"Strat is a true gentleman," said Katie softly. "A fine athlete and a splendid conversationalist. Generous of heart."

Claptrap. The Stratton fellow would be his father's son, gross and sweating. Wax on his mustache and gaudy rings denting his thick fingers. But then, how could poor Katie judge a man? All the men of her acquaintance had been born deformed, become criminal or decayed from disease.

Camilla made a decision. She drank her tea. "How refreshing," she lied. "Is young Mr. Stratton yet in Spain? Does he visit you?"

Katie shook her head. "I had fine jewels, which a friend of Strat's gave me when we were fleeing. We sold them, and with the proceeds, Strat was able to buy passage to Egypt."

But not *your* passage, thought Camilla. "Egypt!" she cried, as if it were wonderful, and not the end of the earth. When young Stratton abandoned somebody, he really completed the job.

Accepting tea had been ever so wise. For now Katie was bursting with truth. "The coming war attracted Strat," she said, leaning forward in excitement. "British troops are even now sailing up the Nile to attack rebels in Khartoum. Lord Kitchener asked for volunteers. Strat hoped to join a camel corps or help build the first desert railway on earth. But! Passing through Spain was the very famous Dr. Archibald Lightner. Of course you have heard of Dr. Lightner's archaeological research."

Camilla had hardly even heard of archaeology.

"Strat managed to make the great man's acquaintance! Dr. Lightner had never had a staff photographer, as he was suspicious of the machinery, but had always used a watercolor artist. When Strat said he would become Dr. Lightner's photographer for no pay, the great man accepted."

Who would accept the gross and disgusting son of Hiram Stratton? Dr. Lightner had probably found out the family connection and was hoping for money. An expedition to chop open a sphinx or a blast into a pyramid must be costly.

Her heart broke watching Katie, who had only death and letters to live for.

"Strat writes often with the details of his adventures," said Katie, fingering the letters as if they were treasure. "He sends me all he earns."

Not likely, thought Camilla, reading the address upside down.

> *H. Stratton*
> *c/o Dr. Archibald Lightner*
> *Road to the Pyramids*
> *Giza*

Katie lifted the letters to her lips and kissed them through the veil. And Camilla knew then that Katie loved Strat the way any girl loves a boy. With all her heart.

# RENIFER:
## IN THE TWENTIETH YEAR OF THE REIGN OF KHUFU, LORD OF THE TWO LANDS

Renifer paused to gaze at the row of bodies staked on poles along the edge of the desert.

The three tomb robbers caught last week had finally died. The priests liked to spear prisoners so the stake traveled all the way up the inside of the body, but did not instantly kill. In this case, the tomb robbers had lived many hours, and one for days. Jackals crept out from the desert by night to chew on the dead men and had not minded eating the feet and thighs of one still alive.

Renifer gave a prayer of thanks that the tomb robbers had been so thoroughly punished.

Then she looked reverently at the just-completed Great Pyramid. How splendid it was, a mountain of shining limestone.

Everybody who lived on the Nile had been part of the Pyramid's creation.

Farmers and potters, fishermen and papyrus makers had the privilege of working on it. They cut and loaded stone, poled barges, dug out the sacred lake, paved the causeway. They baked bread to feed ten thousand workers and sun-dried a million bricks for their houses. They constructed a slideway and ramps to move the massive rocks. They polished the limestone casing, brought flowers for offerings and carried away the sand, one basket at a time. They painted the walls of chapels and the columns of courtyards with a hundred times a hundred portraits of gods, especially their own God. Pharaoh Himself.

The celebrations for the finished Pyramid had lasted for months.

Every man and woman with the strength to greet the morning sun came. They came from Upper Egypt and Lower Egypt, from Lebanon and Punt. They came if they were rich and they came if they were poor. They brought their children and their offerings and their prayers.

They rejoiced at the glory that was Pharaoh, and knelt at His passage when He was borne on His sedan chair, wearing His two crowns.

Twice, Renifer herself had attended Princess Meresankh, Pharaoh's daughter, when the princess brought food to her dead grandmother the queen. Together, royal princess and handmaiden prostrated themselves on the blistering hot silver-faced pavement in front of the queen's chapel.

"Mother of the King," Renifer sang, "follower of Horus, O gracious one, whose every utterance is done for her, daughter of the God's body, Hetepheres, we honor thee."

Afterward, Princess Meresankh actually *spoke* to Renifer, saying how well she sang the chants.

And then the festivities ended, and all Egypt went home.

Pharaoh's barge went back to His palace in Memphis. Shopkeepers sold linen; bakers sold bread. Boys learned to read; girls tended geese. Mothers nursed babies; farmers dug fields.

And tomb robbers, she thought, robbed tombs.

Renifer walked slowly, because it was very hot, one servant girl carrying the fruit they had bought at the market and the other fanning Renifer. Renifer was soon to have her own household and must become experienced in shopping.

Renifer was the envy of every girl she knew. Pankh was strong shouldered and brave. His skin, burnt so dark by the remorseless sun, was like black gold. He was the most handsome and the youngest supervisor of a royal wharf.

Eternal life was fine, and waiting on the princess was fine, but what Renifer cared about was having her own husband, her own house, and as soon as possible, her own children. She was fourteen and it was time.

The doorkeeper opened the big wooden entry set deep in the mud-brick wall. Inside, date palms kept the courtyard cool and shady. Father was reclining under the yellow-and-white-striped awning on the rooftop and Renifer went up the steep ladder to join him. Servants brought bread fresh from the oven and dates still hot from the lowering sun.

Soon the distant sand would turn red and purple with shadow and Pharaoh Himself would be praying for the sun's return in the morning. She would not repeat her own prayers in front of Father, who found religion amusing. Even the Pyramid meant little to Father, who just shook his head when he happened to notice it.

"You look especially lovely today," said her father, "and I think it time to discuss your marriage."

"Oh, yes, Father!" cried Renifer. "Pankh will be here soon. He's taking me to a concert on the wharf."

The days were so hot and glaring that the best entertainments occurred after dark. She helped herself to olives, planning what to wear. She owned much gold jewelry, but neither Father nor Pankh liked her to wear it in public. Sometimes Renifer pouted over that rule.

"Perhaps," said Father, "you should not marry Pankh after all. I can find a more prestigious match, now that you are in Princess Meresankh's favor."

She said dizzily, "But Father! Pankh is ready to bring me home."

Father shrugged. "Why settle for Pankh when you could do better? My grandsons could have noble blood."

Renifer cared more about hot blood, and from what Pankh said and did when they were alone, he could give her all the sons she might want. She tried to dispel her father's hopes. "The princess barely noticed me. She picked me out of a row of girls. Any soprano would do."

"No. The princess has requested you to attend her again next week. Furthermore, Daughter, the princess ordered you to meet her *within the palace walls,* not on the plaza where the musicians gather. You, my daughter, will be in the presence of Khufu, Lord of the Two Lands. The princess wishes you to sing for Him."

Pharaoh Himself would hear her sing?

It was too great an honor. She was not good enough.

And she was not sure she wanted the honor. She wanted to think about having a household, and folding bed linens freshly pressed, and of course making babies. If she had to sing for Pharaoh, she might get scared, and sing badly, and receive punishment, for the Living God must have the best and the first in all things.

She wanted to put Pankh first in all things. That was part of the wedding vow, and she could hardly wait to tell him yet again that he was first in all things.

"Tonight you will stay home with your mother," said her father in the voice that brooked no discussion. "Nor will you be in the presence of Pankh. Tonight or any other night. You can do better. I shall end the engagement."

"I must have misunderstood that statement," said Pankh in a slow deep voice, startling them badly. He was standing on the rim of the roof, hands on hips, feet apart, looming in the dusk like a temple god. His white kilt was bright as moonlight and the gold bands on his arms as thick as jawbones. "Surely, Pen-Meru, you are not thinking of taking your daughter away from me."

"It is not an official agreement, as you recall," said Father dismissively. "Merely a discussion we had. A discussion I will now have with others as well."

Pankh lifted from its pedestal the beautiful small

statue Father had recently acquired of the goddess Sekhmet.

Sekhmet was portrayed as a seated lion goddess; her powers were many and terrifying. She could escort Pharaoh in war, but also sweep the country with disease. She was both love and hatred; both revenge and protection.

This Sekhmet was pure gold and fit for a Pharaoh.

Now Pankh lifted the goddess by her back, as a cat lifts her kittens. He tapped an insolent rhythm on her lion mane.

Father sat very still.

"Renifer is mine," said Pankh softly, "and you, too, Pen-Meru, are mine." He tightened his grip on Sekhmet, as a killer holds the rock with which he will break the skull.

Renifer felt Sekhmet's anger like a spider's web. The goddess's fury was enveloping them all, as when irrigation canals open, and water turns the world into a web of water, and none can pass.

Her father caught his breath. "I was mistaken, Pankh," he said hoarsely. "Of course Renifer is yours. Whenever you wish her."

Renifer could hear the slap of oars on the water of the Nile, the laughter of children playing in the neighbors' courtyards, the rustle of palm leaves in the wind. Her father—Pen-Meru—afraid?

Servants bustled up with torches to be set in their niches, plates of meat and bread and cheese, bowls of stew with barley and chickpeas. Renifer's little sister and brothers, having spent the day playing naked in the sun, came shrieking and giggling for dinner, their nurses running alongside to put robes on them as the air grew chilly.

"Come, Renifer," said Pankh. "The night is beautiful. We will return when it pleases me. Your father will not be talking to other suitors."

Her father was no longer in charge. She might have said her marriage vows already, because Pankh was the one whose permission she needed.

In the streets of Memphis they walked. They said good evening to friends, bought sweets from vendors, listened to a band of flutes, and sat on a bench above the Nile, watching parties on pleasure boats.

"You look lovely in that shawl," said Pankh.

"Father is always coming home with some extraordinary gift," she said nervously. "Pankh? Up on the rooftop? It almost sounded as if you were threatening Father."

"Silly goose," said Pankh. "I just reminded him that I always get what I want."

Renifer was horrified. He was begging a god to lash out and prove him wrong. Or a goddess. "But you treated Sekhmet as a weapon," she whispered. She felt herself at the top of something as high as the Pyramid, and as steep; felt herself falling, and falling with her was a shape so terrible she must keep her eyes closed and her thoughts protected.

"A weapon?" Pankh laughed. "I was just juggling it around." He snapped his fingers to show how little he

37

cared for the goddess. "If I need a weapon, I have a knife."

"But Pankh—"

"I have reached the end of my patience," said Pankh sharply. "I do not care for a wife who questions my decisions."

What decisions? thought Renifer. I don't even know what we're talking about.

"I'm sorry," she said humbly, but she was afraid.

Her father and her beloved were hiding something, using a goddess who would gladly destroy them with one swipe of her immortal paw.

Evil was coming, and Renifer was powerless to get out of its way.

# II

*Time to Fall*

# ANNIE: 1999

Suddenly the special Egyptian exhibition exploded with schoolchildren. Seventh graders, possibly eighth. Filled with the noisy excitement of a field trip, they had not the slightest intention of learning anything. They rattled around the exhibition while their teacher read aloud from placards.

So she was not going to change centuries.

Strat had done that for her. He was here. In her time.

Annie wanted to touch Strat as tenderly as they had touched a hundred years ago. How perfect he still looked. He wore cargo pants and a navy sweater heavily knitted in braids and whorls. He could have been a young sailor from some Irish island, whose sister or mother had been knitting all winter to create this masterpiece. Strat's hair was the same moppy annoying badly cut hair she had known a hundred years ago. He had worn a cute little cap then, the kind men wore when they drove automobiles with open tops and running boards.

Annie had a moment of regret. Other times were so much more exciting and romantic. Neither word could ever be used to describe the suburbs of New York City. She had bought the adventure outfit not to travel into New York, but to travel into 1899. And now she wouldn't get to go.

A yelling knot of boys jostled them, and then an elbowing cluster of girls. Their teacher raised her voice and loudly proclaimed her views of ancient Egyptian art. The class scattered in all directions.

The boy Strat was paying more attention to the photograph than to Annie. Finally he said to Annie, "I think you're right." He smiled in a friendly bland way, only half looking at her. A shock wave went through Annie Lockwood.

*He did not know her.* She was going to have to introduce herself to a boy whose smile and hair and kiss she remembered so well. "What am I right about?" she said weakly. "I don't see Strat in the picture."

"Stratton was the photographer, remember, so he isn't in any of the pictures. But I'm curious. How do you know about Stratton?"

Annie never thought of him as Stratton. To her, he had always been Strat. To a boy who did not remember her, however, she could hardly say, "I used to date you, a hundred years ago." So she said, "I read that Strat left his home in America and went to Egypt."

"Where did you read that?" asked the boy excitedly. "Because our family has tried to find out more about him. You see, Stratton was my great-grandmother's brother. His full name was Hiram Stratton, Jr."

That's what you think, thought Annie Lockwood. *You* are Hiram Stratton, Jr.

Then his words sank in. This boy's great-grandmother was the *sister* of Strat. That would be Devonny. So he wasn't Annie's Strat at all. He had not come through Time. He was nothing but the descendant of a sister. Some distant cousin killing time in a museum. Oh, surely not! Time wouldn't do that to her.

"We have other photos that Stratton took, also in Egypt," said the boy, "but he didn't leave many trails for us to follow. We don't know what happened to him later. What book did you read it in?"

She hadn't read it anywhere. She'd been there. "What is your name again?" she asked.

"They call me Strat. But my real name is Lockwood Stratton."

Annie Lockwood nearly fell over. He possessed *her* last name as *his* first name? That could not be coincidence.

Eighth-grade boys swarmed like hornets around the gold Sekhmet, bumping into Strat's knees and Annie's back.

"We can't concentrate on the exhibition until this class has moved on," said Annie. "Want to go to the museum cafeteria and have a dessert with me? I'd love to hear about your family. You see"—she considered a reasonable lie—"I think we have a photograph of Strat's too."

"You talk as if you know him," teased the boy. "He died a hundred years ago, you know."

"He lived a hundred years ago," Annie corrected him.

They walked down the magnificent stairs, which made Annie feel like a princess in a palace. The boy tapped one of the names incised on the walls: *Hiram Stratton, Sr.* "My great-great-grandfather," he said.

A man Annie had encountered another time. The cruelest man she had ever met. A man who had sworn to destroy his own son—and had. A man who had sworn to destroy the mother of his own children—and had. A man who . . .

Annie's head swam. A veil came between her and the names of the donors. The letters fell off the walls and onto her face like hail, pelting her with memory.

Time opened like a cellar door, for her to fall into blackness.

Hiram Stratton even now was planning to destroy . . . *something . . . someone . . .*

Her feet slipped on the marble steps.

It had been this way before. A first falling, then a second. Then, at last, the step through Time. Scudding across the years like a ship in a high wind.

A guard leaned his face into hers. How antique his features, how dark and wind-beaten his glance. For a moment, the guard stood on the far side of Time. But then he was just a museum employee. Had she skipped breakfast? he wanted to know. He didn't want her to faint and fall on the stone steps and hurt herself.

"I caught her," said the boy, putting his arm around her. Annie knew that hand. The hand on Annie's shoulder was Strat's hand. "She's fine," he told the guard.

"We're on our way to the cafeteria anyway. I'll see she has something to eat."

He pulled Annie to her feet and they walked on together, not touching. Not touching him made her ache. She had known the ache before, too. This was Strat. The real thing. Not a distant cousin.

Time! she called silently. Strat's here. Forget what I asked for. I don't want to change centuries after all. I don't need to anymore. You can leave.

But she had called upon Time too strongly.

Time, having listened, would answer.

# KATIE: 1899

Katie washed out the teacups, which she had borrowed from Mother Superior when she found she had a guest. A guest who offered to save her, bring her home and even provide her with an income!

But with what speed Miss Camilla Matthews had departed. Having squinted at Strat's letters, she was done. She did not care about seeing Douglass, nor did she wish a tour of the hospital.

I trusted her, thought Katie. Here among nuns, I let myself believe that being a woman makes a person good. I, with my childhood! I know that gender does not predict goodness.

Katie beat her fists on the tiny tea table. Then she ripped off her veil and sobbed into her hands. At St. Rafael, she was usually at peace with the Lord and the cruelly formed body into which He had placed her. Now she felt assaulted. This woman—girl, really, hardly older than Katie herself—had connived and lied and encouraged Katie to expose the thoughts of her heart.

It wouldn't be Devonny trying to find Strat. If Strat

46

wished to communicate with Devonny, he could do so—and probably had.

It was Hiram Stratton, Sr., who had enough money and interest to send a woman across the ocean to ply Katie with falsehoods.

Hiram Stratton, Sr., could not tolerate defeat. He did not care who had to be crushed as long as he was the victor. Not only had his one and only son talked back and offered unusual opinions, but then the boy refused to marry Harriett, whose hand Mr. Stratton had chosen for Strat. First among virtues in a son was absolute obedience. When Strat failed to display it, Mr. Stratton put him in an asylum so that his will would be broken.

Katie herself had heard the asylum doctor read aloud the letters he wrote to Mr. Stratton, describing how Strat whimpered and cringed like a kicked dog. But Mr. Stratton had not won, in the end, for by fair means or foul, Strat had defeated both the asylum and his father.

What destruction might come to Strat now, at the hands of this Camilla Matthews?

Katie composed a cable, telegrams being a marvel of technology. Why, this cable would arrive in Egypt long before Miss Matthews could even find a ship! Truly, the nineteenth century was a magnificent time. Katie trembled to think of the twentieth, only weeks away, and what might be invented in those decades.

STRAT. DANGER. MY FAULT. IMMEDIATELY LEAVE EGYPT. YOUR FATHER IN PURSUIT. HIS

AGENT A WOMAN, CAMILLA MATTHEWS.
LETTER FOLLOWS. LOVE KATIE.

She took the carefully printed telegram and more than enough money to cover the cost of sending it to Cairo and went to the gate of the hospital. The gate was not to keep patients in, but to warn strangers away.

She had not left since the day Strat sailed. His letters were her only door to the world. And now, stepping beyond the pale, she remembered the world!

The profile of a Moorish castle and a row of green cedars. An ancient Roman aqueduct against a blue sky and a street market down the hill, full of children and laughter. The clop of horses' hoofs and the clatter of wagon wheels called her name.

What temptation to give up her cause and walk away from her patients into sunshine and safety. Beyond the beautiful city lay a gleaming sea. She herself could carry the warning to Strat. He had been a true friend, such a few on earth ever have.

But if Katie went to him, she would be a burden. Strat would have to figure out what to do with her . . . when there was nothing to do with her.

Katie prayed. The Lord strengthened her.

Then she called out to a friendly-looking passerby. She spoke in Spanish, of course, having learned it easily. She was proud of her accent. "Will you deliver a cable to the telegram office, please? Here is plenty of money, and a good tip as well."

The man pointed to the ground halfway between

them. Katie set down her precious warning, piling coins on top so the wind would not blow the page away. She gave the man God's blessing and returned to the enclosure.

When she had shut the gate behind her, tears assaulted her: for herself and for all ruined lives. And while she prayed for calmness of heart, the man in the street walked on without pausing. Nothing would make him handle what a leper had touched.

A wagon passed by. The wheels sent the coins flying into the dust and tore the cable in half. Later a child found one of the coins and bought food.

# ARCHIBALD
# LIGHTNER: 1899

Archibald Lightner was furious. He had enough to do without having to go into Cairo and rescue his foolish photographer. "I've half a mind to fire you," he said when he finally stomped into the French embassy. "You can't even do a decent watercolor."

"I'm the photographer," the boy protested. "I never said I could paint."

"Well, then, you should be more versatile," snapped Archibald Lightner. His dig was full of stupid people. Of course, he was of the opinion that most people were stupid, but one always hoped to avoid them. Or at least not hire them.

"Actually," said the boy, "you aren't paying me anything."

Dr. Lightner remembered now. Something to do with a leper colony. The boy certainly looked healthy. In fact, he looked perfect. Archibald, who was beaky, gawky and gaunt, had always wanted to look like this young man. Bronze and strong, like a Greek statue. Archibald resembled a heron.

"What is your full name, anyway?" he said irritably. He had searched the boy's possessions, hoping to find a passport, but paperwork was not required at most borders, and it did not look as if the boy possessed any. In fact, other than love letters from a girl named Katie, the boy possessed virtually nothing.

I don't know a thing about him, thought Dr. Lightner. Perhaps I should request that he move on. If I give him money, he will be eager to do so. On the other hand, I pay him nothing, and in exchange he gives me fine photographs.

"I cannot lie to you, sir," said the boy, his cheeks turning red. "I must tell you my full name, although I beg that you not use it. I am Hiram Stratton, Jr."

"Your father is Hiram Stratton?" Archibald Lightner was astonished. He had perceived the camera boy as a servant, just above the natives who toted rubble. Hiram Stratton was one of those astonishing Americans who had achieved inconceivable wealth, and now, bored by wives and mansions, was giving it away. People were lined up, hoping their museum or hospital or library might be handed a vast sum.

Archibald Lightner considered how he might spend a vast sum. Quickly and enjoyably, he decided.

"How is it that the son of Hiram Stratton has no possessions except a change of clothing and a camera?" asked Dr. Lightner. "Are you being fully honest in this matter?"

"My father and I are estranged," said the boy stiffly. "I

do not possess a dime of his, nor do I anticipate a return to his household."

"You will pardon the insult implied by my next remark, Mr. Stratton." (For he could not continue to address the youth as if he were mere staff.) "But when a young son is so deeply estranged, one must wonder if the son committed misdeeds so great that he dare not return to the bosom of his family."

The French, who were always committing misdeeds so great that they dare not return to the bosom of their families, liked Strat better now.

Strat flushed deeply. "I ask you, sir. Is it not possible that the misdeeds were committed by the father? Perhaps the son has chosen a life in which he and his father's misdeeds will not collide."

The French were satisfied. Not only was the young man from a fine family, he cast off wealth as if it mattered not. He was morally above his own parent, refusing to be stained by his father. It was worthy of an opera.

The attaché said, "We accept, *monsieur,* that our two citizens were careless and caused their own deaths. We regret this unfortunate episode here in Cairo, Mr. Stratton." There was bowing and nodding and stroking of mustaches.

They patted the Stratton heir on the shoulder as he left.

Dr. Lightner was not so quick to believe in the boy. All America knew that Hiram Stratton, Sr., had done evil things en route to becoming rich.

The apple, thought Archibald Lightner, does not fall far from the tree. Hiram Stratton, Jr., might travel halfway around the world to escape being his father's son, but he is still his father's son. And that means he has the capacity for evil.

# ANNIE: 1999

In the center of each table in the museum restaurant were folding paper pyramids describing the exhibit. Annie yearned to keep one. Should she ask the waitress and risk being refused, or just quietly fold it up and slip it into her purse?

The tables were jammed next to one another. Inches away, an elderly couple argued hotly about the same problem. "Fine," said the husband testily, "steal one."

His wife glared at him and tucked the paper pyramid into her purse. "It isn't stealing, Albert. It's a souvenir. Besides, lunch was expensive."

"It's stealing," said the husband, as if he might summon New York's Finest, arrest his wife, and be done with it.

The boy was laughing. "That's the thing about marriage," he whispered to Annie. "The decades pile up and so do tempers."

"Tell me about it," said Annie. "But sometimes they rescue themselves. My parents left today on their second honeymoon."

"Really? How nice. Did they get married again and everything?"

Annie nodded. "My mother went on a killer diet so she could fit into her wedding gown again, and Dad into his same tux. My brother was best man and I was maid of honor. We even had the same guests. It was fun in an embarrassing kind of way." She skipped the part about the affair her father had promised to abandon. Who knew whether to believe him? But Mom believed, and it was her marriage.

She said, "I remember that Hiram Stratton, Sr., made a fortune in railroads. I never knew he was a philanthropist." If I could touch your hair, she thought, I would know whether you are my Strat.

But they were sitting opposite each other in a public place and he thought they were strangers. "The family legend is that Hiram Stratton, Sr., disowned Hiram Stratton, Jr., because Junior went insane. Junior took up gentle Victorian activities like watercolors and eventually went to Egypt for a rest cure. He took a few photographs for the Lightner dig and then—who knows?"

They called him Strat, not Junior, thought Annie. And he wasn't insane. He loved me. Of course, my brother, Tod, would call that insane. "So you're Devonny's great-grandchild," she said instead.

"You make it sound as if you and Grandmother Devonny met," he said, laughing.

We did, thought Annie. She sent me on a mission, to save Strat from the asylum. But it went wrong in the end, and we had to part.

"Devonny Stratton married an Englishman," he explained. "They had two children. The older son became an earl or something, but the younger son came back to America and called himself Lockwood Stratton. His son, my father, was plain old Bill Stratton, and now I'm Lockwood Stratton again. Ridiculous British-type name, huh?"

No. Lockwood was not a ridiculous British-type name.

It was a ridiculous American-type name. Annie's.

Annie folded and unfolded the paper pyramid to distract herself. She swallowed her latte. She loved the puffy creaminess and the soft sugar at the bottom. "I'm a Lockwood myself. My name is Annie Lockwood. It would be," she said carefully, "somebody in my family that Devonny got the name from." Because I tried to save Strat, she thought. And maybe I did. I've never really known.

"That is so terrific! Then we're related, in a nonrelated kind of way."

He had Strat's smile. The one that said, This is the best day and you are the best person to spend it with.

The second falling came.

She gripped the tiny restaurant table and did not fall completely. It was more the dizziness that hits anyone from time to time: a skidding of the mind, the tires of your thoughts on black ice. She could not quite see the boy's face, and could not quite remember Strat's, and then it was over, and Lockwood Stratton was studying the bill.

"What's my share?" said Annie thickly.

"Please let me pay. I'm getting a kick out of this. I love that we're both Lockwoods."

# RENIFER:
## IN THE TWENTIETH YEAR
## OF THE REIGN OF KHUFU,
## LORD OF THE TWO LANDS

The great torches along the polished causeway had been lit. The avenue past the temples and up to the Pyramid gleamed in the night. The wind off the desert grew cold.

The tomb robbers held no grudge against Hetepheres. They hoped she would have eternal life. They assumed, however, that she would be fine without her jewels.

They had been robbing her tomb for several nights now, having chipped away the plaster that hid the entrance. Her little mortuary chapel had potted palms and ferns, watered by temple servants. Now there were many more, watered by tomb robbers, which after their night's work, the thieves slid over the stones to hide the forced entry.

They had taken from the tomb most of the smaller items and were now considering how to take the larger ones.

Using levers, they tipped up the lid of the great stone sarcophagus. In it would rest the finest jewels, lying next to and on top of the mummy. The queen's *ka* would be flying around, frantic and angry, but they had been robbing tombs for generations. No man yet had been hurt by a *ka*—only by priests who thought they were above bribery.

It took some time to maneuver the two-ton stone lid out of the way. They balanced it crosswise on the rim of the sarcophagus and hoisted out the light wooden coffin. They removed an immense gold pectoral of vulture's wings, solid with jasper and lapis lazuli. Somebody's wife or daughter would look magnificent in the morning.

Of course, she would have to look magnificent in private, until the gold was melted down and molded into something that could not be recognized. But melting down stolen gold was a daily activity, like baking bread or netting fish.

If Pharaoh caught them, He would have them impaled. But the robbers merely found this exciting. They did not expect Pharaoh to be told. Sufficient bribes had been paid for many nights of privacy. The guardians of the City of the Dead were always happy to receive gold. The priests who served the dead queen her daily meals were also satisfied by gold.

That was the thing about gold. Everybody wanted it and everybody was satisfied by it.

Except when they wanted more.

# ANNIE: 1999

The third falling was hideous and wrong.

Even as it was happening, Annie knew that only bad things could come of this. She would suffer—and worse, she would cause others to suffer.

She saw the boy's eyes open wide, saw his puzzlement.

She tried to call to him, but Time peeled them apart.

Decades ripped at her hair and years tore her skin. She gained velocity. Passing years heaved around her like earthquakes. Annie was screaming, but her voice was torn from her throat by the wind of Time. Her fingertips scraped along centuries, her body bruised by millennia.

*Stop,* begged Annie. *You're taking me too far. If Strat is out there, he's in 1899.*

But she was merely mortal and had no weapons.

Time possessed them all.

# HIRAM STRATTON, SR.: 1899

"Ah, Mr. Stratton," said the museum trustee, "such a delight to lunch with you."

Actually, he found Hiram Stratton appalling. The man had grown so obese from fine food and liquor that his belly jutted into a room like the prow of a tugboat. The immense mustache was groomed and waxed, the teeth yellow from nicotine, and the pipe clenched in the jaw gave off a noxious odor. The eyes were too small for the lumpy face, and blinked too seldom, as with a shark. Below the small beard, the starched white collar was crushed by the weight of jowls and chin.

The museum had opened an American Wing, which embarrassed the trustee, since Americans were not capable of producing art. The museum should contain only *actual* art—Italian oil paintings or Greek statues. Perhaps Mr. Stratton had been coaxed into believing in the existence of American art.

No doubt the man wanted his name on a plaque or a door. The trustee shuddered to think of his beloved museum stained by the name of this family. Must I have anything to do with this revolting person? thought the trustee, resenting his assignment.

"I am thinking," said Hiram Stratton, Sr., "of giving several million dollars to the Egyptian collection."

The trustee was passionate about the Egyptian collection. He loved pyramids and the Nile, papyrus and tombs. He found he didn't care as much about the Stratton name as he had a moment ago. "Archaeology is expensive, dear sir. One must have quite a staff. We, of course, sponsor Dr. Archibald Lightner, who even now is working at the foot of the Great Pyramid. Naturally you have read his gripping books."

Personally the trustee didn't think Mr. Stratton could read. But the man could count. Millions at a time. What that money could do for the Egyptian collection!

And it was imperative to remove antiquities from Egypt swiftly, because the country was making noises about wanting to keep them for itself! Absurd. To think of leaving such treasures with mere Egyptians!

"I wish," said Mr. Stratton, "to visit the excavation prior to making my gift."

The trustee imagined Mr. Stratton flattening little Egyptian donkeys. "How thrilled Dr. Lightner will be to have a man of your stature visit," he lied.

Mr. Stratton had a peculiar request. He did not wish his name used. Dr. Archibald Lightner was merely to know that an important donor was arriving. In fact, Hiram Stratton would arrange his visit through another group entirely. "My dear sir," said the trustee, confused, for there was but one reason to give money—to be applauded by one's friends—"surely you want your name in the papers."

"When one has wealth, one is forced to take precautions," said Hiram Stratton.

In other words, thought the trustee, the factory fire haunts you. Somebody out there would like to cut you to pieces. "It is a sorrowful world," he said, "when gentlemen such as yourself must deal with an ungrateful public."

# CAMILLA: 1899

Camilla was astonished to find that Egypt was over-run by tourists.

She met hunters eager to bag a crocodile, collectors of mummies, explorers of rivers and invalids in sedan chairs hoping to bake themselves healthy. Hordes of British officers were exploring Cairo and Giza and Saqqara before joining the attack at Khartoum.

Camilla pretended that a handsome British officer—no, a *titled* handsome British officer—would fall in love with her and beg for her hand in marriage.

But the British were even shorter than the Americans. Camilla towered over every man in sight.

She had come as a newspaperwoman, Duffie having obtained a fake assignment for Miss Camilla Matthews. Camilla, with a mass of other tourists, approached the Pyramids. The donkey she rode was small and plump and hung with tassels. She had to hold her feet up so they did not scrape the ground.

Nothing had prepared her for the sight of the Pyramids.

She knew there were two million two-ton rocks in

Khufu's Pyramid, but to see them! To gaze up and up and up, stunned by the actual accumulation of all those stones, and each its own color of gold; the Egyptian sun beating down until every angle and corner burned with fire.

Oh, thought Camilla, to have known the man—or god—who thought to build this monument.

The Pyramid was clustered with climbers: two or three natives in billowing white robes vaulting easily from stone to stone, and then reaching out long brown hands to haul up an exhausted and sweating tourist. In every language came their cries of encouragement: *"Allez-y doucement!" "Dem halben-weg!" "Pazienza, signora!"*

The wind lifted sand and flung it in her face, leaving her skin raw and stung. Just so had Camilla flung lies at Katie. Camilla felt as sick in her gut as if she had been drinking from the Nile. Far worse, she had drunk from the example of Hiram Stratton.

She, Camilla Mateusz, had trespassed on a saint.

Life had already used Katie so badly. What right had Camilla to use her?

I had to! Camilla told herself. It was necessary to find the son, and through the son punish the father! I must shrug about it.

But she knew herself to be infected, from her rage toward the father and her daily practice of lying and cheating and conniving for Mr. Duffie.

Camilla strode on. The walking was difficult. The Giza plateau was nothing but sand and stone broken by centuries of weather and feet and by decades of excavation. Her chestnut leather boots were scratched by shards and rubble. Fine clothing was a good thing, but better was a clean heart, she thought.

Quarrying had taken place everywhere, giving the plateau an odd geometry, with so many squares cut away over the millennia. The passage of so much time allowed Camilla to shrug. Who cared about a clean heart? She cared about money, and if it was dirty, so be it. It would still feed her brothers and sisters.

Several hundred feet beyond the Pyramids and the Sphinx was a tent city: headquarters of Dr. Lightner's dig. Fenced off by posts and a single frayed rope, it was guarded by an Egyptian in a long swirling robe of chocolate brown. He was armed—a rifle on his shoulder, a pistol at his waist and a knife literally in his teeth. Camilla loved him. He was treasure and greed, adventure and attack.

Her letter of introduction to Dr. Archibald Lightner—her false letter, designed by Hiram Stratton himself—moved Camilla past the barricade.

The great man sat under an awning and behind a table littered with shards of rock and pottery. He looked at her with dislike, read the letter and sighed. "Miss Matthews, I prefer not to deal with females. Their educations are poor and their presence distracting."

Camilla, whose education was indeed poor, and who planned to be a major distraction, could not argue.

In spite of his opinion of females, however, Archibald Lightner obeyed the rules of courtesy and got to his feet.

And now the word great was appropriate. Archibald Lightner was six-and-a-half-feet tall.

Camilla made an instant decision to marry him.

Plenty of women married for money. It couldn't be worse to choose a husband by height. Of course, age was a problem. He had to be twenty years older than Camilla. Possibly thirty. But who cared? He was taller. "I have never been accused of being low to the ground, sir. And I shall not be a nuisance. I shall be the best publicity you can buy. My article will generate large donations. An archaeologist can never have too much money."

Dr. Lightner laughed. It was a rusty sound, as one who rarely encounters anything comic. Making him laugh was how she would accomplish his proposal of marriage. Camilla gave herself a deadline, as if he were a newspaper article. Three weeks, she said to herself, and he will ask for my hand. She looked *up* into his eyes: the first time in her life that a man's eyes were above her own.

"Miss Matthews," he said reluctantly, "how may I begin your instruction?"

She pointed to the Pyramids. "I want desperately to ascend. I spent the voyage reading about Egypt and have yearned for this moment. Must I hire assistance like other tourists? I am strong and accustomed to playing ball games. Might I climb alone?"

He was puzzled, as if she were a hieroglyph not yet deciphered. "No, madam. A lady mustn't attempt the ascent alone. She might grow fatigued from heat or lose her balance and topple."

Camilla had never lost her balance and toppled; not when her father died; not when she masqueraded as a man; not when she visited a leper hospital. She did not plan to topple from a Pyramid either. But women did not contradict great men, nor receive marriage proposals by being strong.

"I will take you," he said suddenly, surprising her; perhaps surprising himself; definitely surprising his staff, who took a second glance at the female in their midst.

They approached the base of the Pyramid. Camilla touched one of the great yellowing stones. She swayed from the impact of such antiquity. She felt she almost knew the men who had piled these stones. Knew their wives and children, their gods and dreams.

"Are you faint already?" demanded the great man irritably.

"I am overcome not by heat, but by history. Not by weakness, but by strength." Camilla caught Dr. Lightner's arm. "Tell me how the stones were quarried and moved. Tell me who was here. Tell me how they lived."

He stared at her as if she were an artifact. "Put your hat back on," he said gruffly. "Fasten the scarf. You must be shaded from the glare." He tightened the chin strap on his own stiff, wide-brimmed hat and took her hand to help her up. She did need help, as her skirt proved confining. Dr. Lightner could vault easily up to the next level, from whence he would reach down to grip her hand, and lean backward. Up the tautness of his body she would scramble. She felt her arm would be pulled from its socket with every yank. She bruised her shin and banged her elbow, but gave no sign, unwilling to ask for rest.

"From the top, Miss Matthews, you will see for miles because the land is flat and the air so clear. You will comprehend this area as one vast graveyard. You will see the floor plan, so to speak: the causeway, the quadrangles of lesser tombs and the remains of minor pyramids."

Twice he dusted her off, apologizing for the intimacy of this act. Once Camilla dusted him off. She was thorough. She did not apologize.

"Tell me," said Dr. Lightner. "What reading did you do to prepare for this article you will write about me?"

"I began of course with your own three books," said Camilla, having purchased them from American tourists who didn't care if they ever heard another word about Egypt again. "My favorite is volume two, in which you discourse about the current events in Egypt as compared to the upheavals of Egypt's magnificent past."

He said casually, as one to whom the topic is of minor interest, "I am preparing volume four."

"Dr. Lightner! What an honor it would be were I permitted to gaze at your first draft."

They reached the summit. Two or three stones of the

final tier remained, creating shade and seating. It might have been designed for tired ladies and handsome men to rest and eat an orange. Dr. Lightner had a tin canteen hanging at his waist, and they shared sips of water. Her lips rested where his had been and now when their eyes met, his dropped first.

In the distance was Cairo with minarets and towers. Closer were farms of emerald green, split by canals, dotted with camels and donkeys moving down dusty lanes.

Peace descended over Camilla.

It was not possible to think of revenge and rage. Perhaps rage and revenge had once occurred in Egypt, but today it was serene and Camilla was part of the eternally repeating life of that eternal river.

"This is the stage of a great theater, isn't it?" Camilla said softly. "Cairo is the audience. A million people are crammed into the auditorium that is Egypt."

"How beautifully you expressed that." Dr. Lightner pointed to a line as sharp as an edge of paper that divided the green fields from the yellow desert. "Look there. Fields and sand are not friends," he told her. "They march up to each other and neither will surrender. That sand extends from the Nile to Morocco! To the Atlantic Ocean itself."

"I should like to travel from oasis to oasis with my camel train," said Camilla, "and meet the Bedouin."

"Yes! And write an article about it! I will help you arrange it." He took her hand for a different purpose than hauling her upward. He took it, she thought, from excitement. From looking forward to her company. He held her hand flat between both of his, as in Egyptian wall paintings.

An emotion as ageless as revenge entered Camilla's heart. She knew suddenly what could cause a lady to lose her balance and topple.

Falling in love.

# STRAT: 1899

Twice that day, Strat felt the presence of Annie. Twice he reached into thin air, thinking to grasp her and haul her through to him. Twice he caught only the wind.

She is near, he thought, but a year or a century divides us.

He could have wept or screamed or even thrown himself off the Pyramid, but he managed to laugh and go on taking photographs of tourists and saving the money to send to Katie.

The third time he so intensely felt the presence of Annie, he lost his grip on the heavy wooden tripod that held his camera. It tipped to the side, falling heavily against a pile of stones. Oh, no! If his camera were broken . . .

Strat's heart sank.

But what was damaged was the stone.

Impossible. A stick of wood could not break stone. Strat kicked the stone with his boot—and it broke. He picked up a piece and rubbed it—and it turned to white dust in his palm.

It was plaster.

Who would apply plaster to a stone in the desert?

Strat opened his penknife and stabbed experimentally at the stones around him. He was surrounded by plaster. He, Strat, was standing on the entrance to a tomb. Some royal tomb had been camouflaged by that plaster for thousands of years, and *he*—not the brilliant archaeologists! not the scholars! not the historians!—*he,* Strat, had found it.

I'll be famous. I, Hiram Stratton, Jr.—

—but he did not want anyone else knowing he was Hiram Stratton, Jr. Already he felt vulnerable and anxious, because Archibald Lightner knew the truth. What if word spread?

Father, thought Strat ruefully, you have truly followed me to the grave. Luckily, it isn't *my* grave. And though I dare not take credit, for publicity would tell you where I am, at least I can take photographs.

He could not wait to tell Dr. Lightner. He ran across the sand and rubble to the dig and saw, several hundred yards away, Dr. Lightner talking with a tall slim girl in a long romantic skirt.

*Annie had come.*

The other night when he climbed to the top of the Pyramid, he *had* reached her. Time *had* let his prayer cross the century.

His body leaped forward and his heart followed. He soared toward her, as an eagle soars on rising heat. He plunged over the crevasse where some archaeologist was digging in the hope of finding a buried tomb ship. He raced over trenches where yet another hoped to find a queen's tomb. He could not slow his steps and he certainly could not slow his heart.

And when he arrived, plunging down a slope, leaping from rock crest to sand hill, he saw that the girl had blond hair.

Annie's was dark.

# CAMILLA: 1899

"Let us descend," said Dr. Lightner at last. "There is work to do."

Down was easier than up. There were fewer occasions on which it was necessary to cling to each other. Camilla could not bring herself, an athlete, to pretend she needed help when she did not.

Halfway down Dr. Lightner said, "Tell me what sort of ball games you delight in."

She was touched that he had been paying attention to her from the first. "Basketball. Have you ever had the pleasure?"

"Oh, yes! We play basketball here for amusement. My young men all played for their colleges. How your team must relish you! You are so magnificently tall."

Camilla stared at Dr. Lightner's weathered face. Sun had burned it to bronze and split it in cracks.

They walked slowly toward the tents, finding much to say. How marvelous to be with a man who was not letting go of her hand. How marvelous, in fact, were hands.

A boy about Camilla's own age suddenly came bounding and yelling toward them.

Camilla was pretending to be thirty, which seemed like the right age for a seasoned reporter sent halfway across the world to write about scientific events, but in fact, she was seventeen. The boy too had the air of somebody pretending to be older, but in fact, still in his teens.

She had the oddest sense that he was racing toward *her*. That they knew each other. She even had the thought that she shocked him; that he was not prepared for the sight of her.

It was not until he pulled up next to them, breathless and excited, that Camilla saw he was astonishingly handsome and very unkempt. His jacket was in desperate need of button reattachment and his trousers needed mending.

"Dr. Lightner! Sir!" he cried. "I have found an undiscovered tomb."

Camilla laughed out loud at this pathetic claim. It was surely the daydream of every tourist: I'll stoop down, find pottery with hieroglyphs, kick away a rock and expose a tomb, which will be filled with gold.

"I knocked over my tripod whilst preparing my camera," said the boy. "The wooden legs are heavy and topped with brass casings. They hit against a desert stone and when I looked, it was not stone at all, but plaster camouflaged as a rock!"

Dr. Lightner quivered. "Perhaps I should take a look."

He and the boy walked with measured pace, though Camilla thought they wanted to fly through the air, dive into the sand and come flailing to the surface with their arms full of Egyptian gold.

In moments, the entire expedition was trooping along, whispering and wondering. What a gathering of fine young men! Camilla gathered that these were intellectuals from the great universities of the world, taking six months or a year to indulge a passion for archaeology. She wondered what it could be like to have the money to do such a thing.

"What is the significance of the plaster?" she asked one of them.

"In my studies at Yale," he told her, "I learned that in ancient times, the entry to a tomb was often disguised with plaster dyed to match the desert."

It did not seem to Camilla it had been necessary to wedge Yale into the response. She decided that she, in turn, would wedge an important women's college into the conversation, as if she too recalled tidbits from otherwise dull lectures.

"You are a lucky reporter, Miss Matthews," said one of the young men. "A real scoop. What an article you will write!"

Camilla was horrified. She didn't know a thing about reporting. She had planned to fake all that.

"What newspaper are you from?" asked the Yale man. "Boston?" he said. "New York?" It had to be one of these; no other city mattered.

"I'm from Kansas," she said, preparing to hand him

the fake card she had had printed up to support her fake credentials.

They burst into uproarious laughter at the idea that people in Kansas could read, or even printed newspapers.

Furious and embarrassed, Camilla took pad and pencil from her satchel and pushed her way to the front. Ladies did have a few advantages in this world. No man would think of pushing back.

A few taps of the chisel and it was established that behind the plaster were flat stones, easily dragged aside, and below them . . . a man-made rectangle. The entrance, perhaps, to the shaft of a tomb.

Dr. Lightner stood for the boy to photograph him above the unopened site. He contained his excitement poorly. He could not stay motionless for the lengthy time a photograph required.

Camilla found she had already written three paragraphs.

The removal of rubble from the shaft began.

The Egyptians were told to work faster, but that did not occur. They had a tempo. They did not rush. After all, thought Camilla, the rocks have been there five thousand years. It's Americans who rush.

Long before they had made much progress, the shadows were too thick for work to go on. People sighed, agreeing to leave the rest for the morrow, and went sadly and separately to their tents.

Camilla, however, approached the boy. She was amazed by his physical beauty. Burnished by the

Egyptian sun, the youth shone. He had retreated over the sand, and was facing the Sphinx, but his thoughts were clearly on a tiny envelope in his hand.

The envelope was not two inches long, the color of an American sky before an autumn storm: gray with tints of angry yellow. He held it to his lips. It was not a kiss, more a communion.

*Communion.*

She was Camilla Mateusz again, thinking of all the Sundays in this wicked year in which she had not gone to Mass and had not taken Communion and had not been a good person. Her eyes blurred with shame.

The boy put the envelope in his shirt pocket, so that it lay over his heart. Uncertainly, Camilla interrupted and was met by a sweet half-smile.

"Might we sit upon one of the Pyramid stones and talk to each other?" asked Camilla. "If you are willing, tell me the details of your discovery for my article."

They circled the Sphinx. The serpent charmers had packed up, the watermelon vendors were sold out and the tables of souvenirs had vanished. The boy took her arm as if they were off to a dance, and they walked over a vast pavement, tilted now by the ravages of Time, and arrived at Khufu's Pyramid.

The best spot was several stones up and they climbed together. "Girls can't usually swing up like that!" he said respectfully. "I've known only one."

"What was her name?" asked Camilla.

"Annie." His voice was so soft she could hardly hear. He traced the outline of the tiny envelope in his pocket.

"What is that in your pocket?" she asked. Working for Duffie had destroyed her inhibition against asking about people's private lives. She must remember that ladies did not pry. Of course, reporters always pried. Perhaps she could not be both.

He answered with courtesy. "Once, long ago, I loved a young lady. We left each other. There was no choice in the matter. All I have of her, and all I ever will, is a lock of her hair."

He carried that girl's token against his heart. Camilla's own heart was assaulted. Would any man ever feel that way toward her? She could not prevent a prayerful vision of herself and Dr. Lightner together, and had to blush at such foolishness. A great scholar? Interested in a half-educated girl, half his age, pretending to be a reporter?

Perhaps she really could be a reporter. Then there would be one true thing in her life. She would not entirely be a tissue of lies. "You and I were never introduced," she said. "I must have your name for my article so that you may receive credit for finding the shaft. I am Miss Camilla Matthews, newspaper reporter from Kansas."

"Really?" he said with interest. "Tell me about Kansas."

Camilla had never been west of New York City, so her answers lacked validity, but Strat repeated her words carefully. He would probably carry them around all his life.

"This has been a lovely night," he said then. "Allow

me to escort you to the tent that Dr. Lightner has arranged for you, Miss Matthews."

"I still do not know your name, sir."

"You need not use my name in your article, Miss Matthews."

She was astonished. "This discovery could be your future."

He shook his head, not interested in his future.

"What shall I call you then, since I am to stay at your camp for some time?" She extended her hand, firmly and in a masculine fashion, so he would not become confused and think she wanted to lean on him.

"People call me Strat," he said finally.

The son of the man who had murdered her father shook Camilla's hand.

# III

*Time to Fear*

# ANNIE

Reeds as thick as Annie's wrist, but unnaturally shaped in triangles—like no plant on earth she had ever heard of—towered around and above her. Lacy fronds and leaves closed out the sky. Fat roots fondled the mud in which they grew, and the mud caught her toes and sucked at her heels.

Birds shrieked. Water lapped. A cloud of purple dragonflies needled past and a frog vaulted out of the water, its wet skin brushing her ankle.

Annie had never known such heat. Sweat poured off her, soaking through her clothes. A white-winged heron rose languidly in front of her, as if half-asleep; as if all creatures, herself included, could not fully waken in this heat.

Gripping the heavy stems—trunks, almost—of the reeds, she tried to find her way out. Out of what? she thought, trying not to sink into terror as she was sinking into mud. Into what?

Leaves as hot as if they had been fried slapped her in the face. The air was so thick with moisture that no matter how deeply she breathed, she failed to find enough oxygen.

"Strat!" she screamed, for he must be here. The only reason Time had hurled her here—wherever she was—was to find Strat.

Nobody answered.

Huge rotting plants rimmed the edges of deep water. She could find no land, no solid earth. To break through these reeds would take a machete. The clothing bought in hope of an adventure was drenched and stinking and the wonderful shoes full of mud and probably leeches, even now sucking on the bottoms of her feet.

In front of her, the water turned gray, developed slick spots and heaved. Two bulging eyes stared at Annie. A pink mouth as large as a trash can opened up and the beast bellowed, its fat teeth as big as her palm.

When it sank back down, a wave lashed up and soaked Annie to the knees.

A hippopotamus. Not the sweet little blue pottery hippo sold in the museum shop. The real thing. The real hideous and dangerous thing.

Annie thrashed around, screaming for help.

Any help. Any people, from any time.

But only the hippo returned to stare at her.

# LOCKWOOD STRATTON

The boy named Lockwood Stratton had never had a fainting spell, nor ever been dizzy, nor ever needed glasses.

Now he seemed to be struggling with all three.

His fingers shivered over the white tablecloth. He concentrated on figuring the tip and putting the bills down. What he had just seen—or not seen—was strange, but more strange was that he had come to the museum at all.

He had no interest in his family background. Any mention of ancestors and he fell asleep or left the room, moaning. And yet when he had read the article about the Egyptian exhibition (he, who never read anything, not even his assignments!), he thought: My ancestor was the photographer at that dig.

His mother would have been thrilled that her son was having a cultural moment.

His father would have been astonished that he even remembered from whom he was descended.

But he had not told them. He had come into the city

alone. Nobody did that. What fun was it to be alone in New York?

Well, I'm not alone now, he said to himself.

He and this Annie Lockwood would go back upstairs and finish seeing the special exhibition. How amazing that she and he shared a name and a history.

"Well, let's head on back," he said cheerfully, although he was not cheerful. He was still shaken by the way she had—but it was impossible. He had not seen that, because it hadn't happened.

"We still have half the exhibition to look at," he told her.

Nobody answered.

In fact, when he forced himself to raise his eyes from the tablecloth and look around, nobody was there. Not Annie, not the couple arguing at the next table, not even a waiter. The restaurant was empty and quiet. He walked uneasily toward the exit. He saw Annie Lockwood nowhere. She was distinctive, with that falling black hair.

She's got to be right here, he told himself. Waiting for me in the hall.

But she wasn't.

He saw the sign for the ladies' room, so he sat on a bench with some other men and waited patiently. But she didn't come out.

Great. I've lost her. Maybe she lost me, too, and she's gone back to the exhibition looking for me.

So he trooped back up the Grand Staircase, but she was not there.

He was embarrassed by how upset he was. Had she fallen into his life, full of delight and stories and lovely dark hair he yearned to touch, and he was so boring she just got up and left?

Although what he had seen was not exactly getting up and leaving.

He circled the special exhibition, pausing at the photograph under which he and this Annie Lockwood had met. The photograph seemed different. As if somebody had been added, or subtracted.

Impossible, he said to himself, shaking off a return of the dizziness that had struck in the restaurant.

He heard Annie scream for help, and he swerved, eyes wide open, to see where it had come from, but the room was empty, except for a guard who stared at him with a strange heavy-lidded antique look.

She went downstairs to the regular Egyptian collection, he told himself. I'll find her at the Temple of Dendur, sitting by the reflecting pool.

# RENIFER

Pankh poled the little skiff through the papyrus reeds while Renifer sang.

Fat pads of lotus swirled by, while brick-red swallows dipped and swerved in their quest for bugs. The hoopoe, a bird Renifer loved beyond all others, followed them, jumping from one papyrus frond to the next. Once she saw the snout of a crocodile, and, distantly, she heard the shrieks of baboons.

Renifer had had the servants put together a picnic basket and she fed Pankh dates and they drank sweet fig juice from the same bowl. She offered him cold duck and he nibbled the meat right down to her fingers. They dipped bread in salted oil and shared a block of cheese.

Twice he kissed her, and the reed boat trembled as they fought for balance, both physical and emotional. He was so handsome. When she looked at Pankh, she could think of nothing but marriage and the joy it would bring. Father, however, had lost his joy in the coming event. He was quiet. He was, in fact, fearful.

What could it mean?

Marriage must not be entered into lightly. She must

be sure of Pankh, and he of her. So Renifer said to him, "We must talk of important things."

He had to laugh at the idea that girls had important things in their lives. He poled into the swamp until the papyrus towered above them, six and eight and ten feet of strong triangular stalks, the wide flat heads darkening the sun.

"You are the most beautiful girl in Egypt," said Pankh. "I am all that is important to you. I will give you everything."

"But what I want, Pankh, is the truth. Tell me what is between you and Father."

"That is between men, Renifer. Men make choices in life. Your father has made his. He will live with them or he will die with them. It is not your place to consider truth or lack of truth. It is your place to obey. Yesterday you obeyed your father; from now on, you will obey me."

Renifer had stopped listening to him. She was watching the most amazing terrifying thing she had ever seen. A spirit was materializing before her. First there was mist. Then shape. Then color and movement.

It was a *ka*.

Renifer had known all her life, and worshiped the fact, that the *ka* returned one day to the body. That was why it was necessary to save the corpse. Without a body, no *ka* could find its way home. But she and Pankh were deep within a jungle of papyrus. There could be no body buried here. The *ka* was lost.

Renifer could think of nothing more dreadful. She

prayed that the *ka* would depart without touching them. Its shape was thickening now, and taking on human form, creating its own body, here in the papyrus! Renifer gazed in awe and terror.

Pankh, realizing he had lost his audience, turned to look where she looked.

"It's a lost *ka*," whispered Renifer, so frightened she could not think what god to call upon.

But the *ka* saw them and cried out.

"Hetepheres," whispered Pankh. He fell to his knees and the reed boat, fortunately stable and hard to sink, shuddered under the weight of his collapse.

How could it be the *ka* of Hetepheres? wondered Renifer. Why would the name Hetepheres even enter Pankh's mind? She has been dead for a year. Besides, the queen was buried so well and so richly. If ever a *ka* had a good place to return to, it is the queen's tomb.

"Go home!" Pankh yelled at the *ka*. "Get away from us!"

But if it were a *ka*, it did not appear Egyptian. It came closer, and the tears it wept were real tears. It smelled bad, as foreigners did.

Renifer decided to treat it as she would a sacred animal—an ibis, or a cow dedicated to Hathor. The first thing was to feed it. She held out a date in the palm of her hand and in her other hand, a cup of fig juice, although it was doubtful that a creature so primitive would know how to drink from a cup, any more than a cow would.

But the creature seized the cup, drinking noisily, and

then bit down hard on the date. It seemed astonished that the date contained a pit and spat the whole thing out. Renifer gave the creature bread instead, and it consumed the bread like a wild dog. Then it stood panting and whimpering.

Pankh had calmed down. "I don't think it's a *ka*," he said. "Maybe a slave girl in the dress of her native land? She has run away, perhaps, and is trying to hide in the papyrus swamp."

How frightening to be lost here! Papyrus was delicate with arching fronds, forming hieroglyphics of their own against the brown Nile and the blue sky. But millions of them . . . mile upon mile of them . . . and they interlaced like prison walls. Feet sank into mud and roots clung to ankles and crocodiles sprang out of dark water. No wonder the poor thing was frightened.

Its clothing was stranger than Renifer had seen even in the slave bazaar. Egyptians did not normally have slaves. Their servants were not sold in streets. Slaves were prisoners of war, and came from distant places that must be thrashed until they understood Egyptian superiority.

But Pankh was correct about the creature being female, and probably also that it was foreign, for its skin was as pale as bleached linen. It looked unhealthy to Renifer. Its hair was very long and must be very hot.

The creature tried to grab the pole with which Pankh pushed the little boat through the reeds but he jerked it out of her reach. "Pankh!" said Renifer severely. "We have to rescue her."

"No, we don't. It isn't a pet," said Pankh. "Don't touch it."

Renifer paid no attention to him. "It's all right," called Renifer, reaching toward the creature. "You may get in the boat with us. I'm going to take you home and bathe you. Don't be afraid. We won't leave you in the swamp."

Renifer held out her arms and the girl came, and Renifer felt its heartbeat, the heat of its skin and the wet of its tears.

Pankh kept the boat pole between himself and the pale creature. "Her skin is the color of a worm from under a rock," he said in distaste. "Perhaps that's the color of a returning spirit."

"Now, Pankh. You just said she was an escaping slave. She cannot be both." Renifer coaxed the girl to sit in the bottom of the boat. She picked out a sweet pastry and the creature ate it, but refused the beer, which looked fine to Renifer, although maybe it needed to be strained again. Nile beer was rather thick. "The gods have sent her to us, Pankh. They even made you cry out the name of Hetepheres. She is not a *ka,* but perhaps sent by the queen's *ka*! I cannot imagine the purpose. But soon the gods will reveal all. Our task will be made clear to us."

"It is clear to me," said Pankh, "that we should leave her here."

Renifer patted the girl's hand and said soothingly, "We're going to go home now. You're going to have a nice bath and put decent clothing on."

"She's the color of a rat's tail," said Pankh.

"She's the color of ivory," said Renifer. Even Pharaoh possessed little ivory, for it was so precious and rare. Father, of course, in his wealth, had acquired a number of pieces. Renifer lifted her voice to the gods and sang a song of thanksgiving for being honored with a girl of ivory.

Pankh swore at the same gods. He poled much more vigorously out of the papyrus than he had coming in.

The creature—or runaway slave—or foreigner—or *ka*—slid into the bottom of the boat and slept.

# ANNIE

Humans!

Annie rushed forward. They were in a funny little boat with a swan's neck prow. But the people in the boat did not want her, and the man shoved her away with his oar.

"No, no," she said desperately. "There are crocodiles in there. Take me with you. Please? I'll do anything."

The man continued to push her away, but the girl behind him suddenly smiled at Annie, elbowed the man aside and drew Annie into the safety of the funny little boat. She was desperately relieved to have her feet out of the mud.

Her rescuer was younger than Annie. Very pretty, with rich warm golden-brown skin. Her black hair was extremely decorative, in many tiny tight braids, falling evenly to her shoulders, and heavily laced with beads. The man was bare except for a white kilt.

The boat was a sort of glorified raft. It was made, Annie realized, of hundreds of the very triangular reeds which had so terrified her. The woven reeds were dried out and stiff, and when she pressed her fingernail into them, they felt like Styrofoam, not wood.

"Papyrus," said the girl, smiling at Annie.

# RENIFER

Once home in the women's quarters, Renifer could not get the girl to remove her dreadful clothing and Renifer could not figure out how to remove it herself. It was tied together in some bizarre foreign way.

The servants were laughing too hard and were also too afraid to be of any use.

Whatever tribe the girl came from, it was very primitive. Clearly, she had no acquaintance with gold or adornment. Her ears were pierced, so at some time in her life, she had worn something. But the only jewelry she possessed now was a plain leather wrist strap with a speckled circle.

Renifer decided on gold for a bribe.

Offering jewelry, one piece at a time, she coaxed the girl into a bracelet, and then a necklace and then another. Finally, Renifer got her to remove the strange clothing. The top piece gripped by means of little circles stuck through holes. It had sleeves, such as Renifer had seen on warriors from the Far East, when they had been captured by superior Egyptian forces.

What a relief to strip the girl naked and scrub away

her foreign smell and dress her in clothing through which the cleansing desert air could pass.

When at last she was clean and well oiled—a process she resisted rather vigorously—Renifer chose one of her finest gowns. They had a clash over how the dress hung, as the girl wanted it to cover her upper body. Renifer tried to demonstrate that breasts were a girl's best asset and the girl of ivory had a fine pair, and must display them. In fact, Renifer had makeup for them, but when she tried to apply it, the girl flung herself across the room and even handed back the gold.

Renifer could only laugh and put the girl in a dress that hung from the shoulders.

Renifer decked the girl in her very finest jewels, the ones Father had acquired during the last year, which she wore only at private dinners, because Father said they mustn't let neighbors realize how successful he had become. The necklace had a swollen solid gold collar from which hung gold lace and intense blue lapis lazuli. The finger rings were shaped like coiled serpents and sacred beetles. The earrings were paper-thin plates of hammered gold, six inches across.

When she was finally dressed, she no longer looked like a fish rotting on the shore. She was almost attractive. Once her face was properly made up, she might even be rather lovely. Renifer had never seen anything quite like her.

"A goddess sent you," said Renifer softly. "I'm sure of it. Tomorrow morning, or perhaps by the setting sun, the goddess will tell me your purpose."

Renifer's nurse sniffed. "She looks like a sacrifice. She is white like the best oxen and you have dressed her in white, like the best priestess. I think she is here to die."

They stared at her, while the pale girl herself stared at her new jewelry.

Renifer shivered, wondering to whom and for what the creature would be sacrificed.

# ANNIE

All her life, Annie had loved those paintings of Egyptian women, their sloe eyes, dark lids and romantic mysterious glances. Renifer painted her just like that, the makeup going from the corners of her eyes all the way back into her hair. Annie sat and enjoyed it. She wasn't even trying to talk. The sounds Renifer made—if in fact her name was Renifer; it could just as easily be Zrnykr or Bjzhirhoo—did not sound like language.

Annie felt oddly as if she had not changed millennia; these were just girls gathered in a girl's bedroom, playing dress-up, putting on new makeup and sharing hairstyles.

Whereupon Renifer took off her hair.

Annie nearly screamed. Renifer was bald. She shaved her head!

Renifer laughed and pointed through a shuttered window at the huge yellow disk of the sun.

They shave their heads to keep cool, thought Annie, and wear wigs to keep off the sun, the way I'd wear a baseball cap. "Don't even think about shaving off my hair," said Annie. "Bad enough you put me in a see-through dress with nothing on underneath it."

Renifer and her maids burst into giggles at the duck-quacking sound of Annie's language. Then she tied Annie's hair into a knot on top of her head to get rid of it, while a servant brought out a magnificent wig.

It was a deeper black than Annie's real hair, with hundreds of the tight twisted braids like the ones in Renifer's wig. Into the wig, Renifer and the serving girl worked a series of gold ornaments, and then Annie was permitted to stand.

She knew by the delight on their faces that she was beautiful; that they were pleased.

Finally, Renifer decked Annie in gold necklaces. In Annie's world, a gold necklace was a slender thread, a mere suggestion of gold. Ancient Egyptians were not so restrained. The necklace Renifer fastened around Annie's throat was splendid. Its weight astonished her.

The wig and the eyepaint had the nice result of making her feel invisible, the way you felt behind sunglasses. You could see other people, but they couldn't see you. And this was a good thing, because Renifer took Annie's hand and led her into a garden and displayed her in the sheer dress.

The garden was enchanting. The dark plumes of palm trees bowed in the evening breeze. Against a tawny mud-brick wall stood an ancient sycamore, bark peeling into leopard spots. Acacia were powdered with yellow blooms. There were oleander, and limes, and roses blooming as if for a score of weddings.

Every tree and shrub stood inside its own little puddle of Nile water. Gardeners were walking about refilling the puddles. Outside each puddle, the dirt was as hard and dry as wooden planks.

Geese and ducks wandered. A cat sunned itself on a wall. Annie's gown was pleasantly cool against her skin. Renifer led her up a ladder to a roof garden. From here, Annie could see children playing tag, leaping from rooftop to rooftop. Men in the street below were coming home from work—fishermen with their catch; vendors with their wagons. They wore cotton nightgowns, like baggy T-shirts to the ankle.

On the desert horizon, Annie saw two pyramids. She caught her breath. Every picture she had ever seen showed three. It didn't precisely tell her the year, but it did tell her the time: She had arrived in Egypt before the third pyramid had been built. What had she just read on the plaques in the museum? Had not Khufu built his Pyramid around 2500 B.C.?

She tried to think how Strat fit into this and realized that she was going to find Strat, here in antiquity. How he must be rejoicing at his good fortune! What archaeologist has not dreamed of falling through Time to the very place he digs?

Annie turned away from the sights of Memphis to find Renifer's friend Pankh—the one-syllable name was easy to learn—staring at her with loathing. He stepped back when she approached, rubbing his arms, as if she literally made his skin crawl. Annie stuck close to Renifer. Pankh wore a pleated white cloth tied diaper-fashion between his legs. To Annie, he appeared comical, but Renifer certainly admired him.

A man who seemed to be Renifer's father greeted them, raising his eyebrows at the sight of Annie, but shrugging. When Pankh's back was turned, the father sent him looks. Just so had Annie and Tod looked at the woman with whom their father had had that affair. If looks were sharp knives, the woman would have died a quick death.

So, thought Annie, Renifer's father hates Renifer's boyfriend.

There was no time to dwell on this interesting problem, because a little sister and several brothers came pounding up the steps to the roof patio, and surrounded Annie, patting her as they did their pet goose and their pet monkey. The children were naked and dusty and beautiful and she found herself laughing and romping with them.

For dinner, there were roast pigeons with onion. There was baked perch with pomegranate sauce. The bread was delicious and also sandy, as if they had made the bread outside on a windy day. There were cakes drizzled with honey and many kinds of cheese.

Annie began nodding off, a giggly little brother on each side of her keeping her upright. Renifer led her away. She was so tired she could hardly make it down the roof ladder.

Renifer's bedroom was so full of beautiful objects. Every possession looked worthy of a king's tomb, but it was the bed Annie wanted to try out. It was wood framed and tilted toward the feet, with a footboard to keep Renifer from sliding off and one of those wonderful wooden pillows, like a torture rack.

But Annie did not get a bed or even a wooden pillow. Mats kept under Renifer's bed were unrolled and all Annie had for comfort was an inch of reed on a mudbrick floor.

She meant to stay awake for hours, memorizing all she had seen so she could tell Strat, but she fell asleep the moment her cheek touched the mat.

She did not know that when the servants unrolled their mats, tiptoeing around her, they carefully placed amulets on all four sides of her, to protect themselves.

# CAMILLA

The following morning, the shaft which young Stratton had discovered was speedily emptied, but spirits sank as soon as the first person descended. The space below was small and unadorned. There were no gilt ceilings. No fine statues. No fabulous treasure. There were the remains of furniture, the wood having disintegrated, only the gold leaf which had wrapped each leg or arm still there. The only other object in the tomb was a huge unopened stone sarcophagus, sealed in antiquity.

"That means," the Yale man told Camilla, "that the tomb was robbed of anything easily carried, while the big pieces were abandoned."

"But surely, if the sarcophagus is sealed," Camilla protested, "there will be a coffin inside. A king's mummy and lots of gold."

"Nothing is for sure in ancient Egypt," said Dr. Lightner ruefully. He was lowered by rope down the sharply slanted shaft. Strat followed, carrying his camera equipment.

Camilla stared down the opening through which Hiram Stratton's son had just disappeared. If only he would rot down there. If only some tomb curse would close in upon him, smothering him with rocks. Then Hiram Stratton would find out what it was like to lose somebody he loved!

She sipped warm water from her canteen, wishing there were a way to keep drinks cold. To make ice, perhaps. She tried to imagine a method of creating ice in hot weather but gave up.

Dr. Lightner emerged from the shaft. He was excited and happy. "Look at this!" he cried.

He sounded like one of her little sisters or brothers bringing home some treasure found on the sidewalk. A bright penny or a lost pencil. Camilla was touched.

He held in his hand something that had been buried thousands of years ago. For the first time, it was struck by sun.

It was a sandal of gold.

Camilla had rarely seen gold. The gleam astonished her. No wonder the world had fallen in love with this metal; no wonder that conquistadors and pirates, presidents and archaeologists wanted it. She wanted that sandal. She was amazed by the ferocity of her desire. She asked permission, and received it, to touch the shoe. But when she did, a strange damp terror crept into her and she pulled her hand back as if from a hot iron.

"It was lying on the floor," said Dr. Lightner. "Just one sandal. Not the other. It's solid gold. Not intended for actual wear."

"Yet it was worn," said Camilla. "See? The sole of the sandal is scraped."

They stared in astonishment. She was right. The sandal had once slid onto the bare foot of an Egyptian girl, its intricately designed gold rope between her toes.

It was an Egyptian Cinderella's slipper, thought Camilla. She was leaving the ball, and her magic slipper fell off and was left behind. Somewhere in time, she still wears her other slipper.

Dr. Lightner held the gold sandal against his cheek, to feel its history. "Would the slipper fit you, Miss Matthews?" he asked.

"It was made for a small and slender foot," she told him. "My foot is far too large. You will have to find a princess."

"Miss Matthews, say no such thing. Among women, you are a queen."

Camilla blushed and then, being truthful, extended her right foot. Grinning, he stuck his out next to it. Dr. Lightner's feet made her own look delicate. They stood in each other's footprints, lost their balance, and gripped each other to keep from falling. Before it could become impropriety, of course, they stepped back and pretended to be doing other things.

"Might I descend the shaft?" said Camilla eagerly, merely being polite, not expecting to need permission.

But Dr. Lightner refused. She was a lady, he explained.

On the one hand, Camilla loved being a lady: too important to take risks or get dirty. On the other hand, she hated being a lady: too *un*important to participate in the fun.

The mystery of the tomb, however, was not so much the single sandal, but its owner. When torches were brought into the depths, and the hieroglyphs on the stone coffin read, it turned out to be the sarcophagus of Hetepheres, mother of Khufu, who built the Great Pyramid.

Impossible. This little hole—a queen's tomb?

Pharaoh forced his people to labor for decades to create *his* tomb—and stuck his mother into an undecorated closet?

"Surely, inside that sarcophagus lies the queen herself," said the young man from Yale.

"How fabulous her mummy will be!" said the boy from Princeton.

Dr. Lightner spread his hands in a shrug. "One does not know these things in advance. Egypt likes to hold her secrets."

"We must have a ceremony for the opening of her sarcophagus," said the youth from Harvard, having been raised to expect things to go his way, "and invite all the important archaeologists in Egypt. Within easy reach are scholars and dignitaries from Germany and Austria, France and Italy, America and England."

The site was chaotic as dusk fell. Egyptian workmen scurried and carried. Men from other digs in Giza came to discuss the find and the possibility of treasure. Camels spat and donkeys bellowed. The shadow of the Pyramid sketched a black line over the sand.

Camilla kept track of every member of the expedition.

The moment finally came in which nobody was looking in her direction. Camilla felt the nuns who had taught her calling *Stop it!* She ignored them.

She wrapped the gold sandal in her scarf and drifted away.

All the action was around Hetepheres' tomb. She walked swiftly to the long low tent where young Stratton and the college boys slept.

She was now a thief. She could never deny that in this life, and in the next life, she must face her Maker, and when asked which commandments she had broken, she would have to admit that she had stolen.

But Hiram Stratton, Sr., had stolen a life.

There were five cots in the tent, each with some gear stacked by. Which was Strat's? By the bed closest to the door, on a small scarred wooden trunk, lay one of Dr. Lightner's volumes with a folded letter half-tucked into it. Camilla withdrew the letter.

*Dear Katie,*

*Your letters continue to make me feel worthless and self-indulgent. I participate in the opening of tombs— and you serve the most wretched humans on earth. That sickness terrifies me, Katie. One day, I fear, you will be what they are. And yet you chose that life. I will never understand. But I will always be proud.*

*I sold my best photograph of the Sphinx to a London newspaper! I had to keep a bit of money to resole my boots; sand is hard on footgear. But here is the rest. Katie, buy vegetables and milk, so you resist illness. Go ahead, laugh. You know I despise vegetables and milk. But I worry. You might spend this on chocolate for your patients, instead of upon yourself.*

*Today we descend into the tomb I found! Pray I will take a photograph good enough to sell. Then I will have lots of money to send you.*

*Your very dear friend,*
*Strat*

Camilla stood for a moment. Then she opened the trunk.

Strat had few possessions. A spyglass, that he might see across the desert. Notebooks and pens. A few changes of clothing and linen. A Bible, with a red ribbon marking his place.

She lifted the Bible, intending to see what book and chapter he was reading, but out fell the tiny envelope. It was not sealed, but the flap gently tucked in. Camilla opened it, too. The lock of hair Strat had told her about was black and shimmery as silk. It was very straight and did not want to be in such a small space, but leaped toward the opening, straightening itself as if it still lived and grew.

*Annie,* thought Camilla, and the dank terror that had come through the gold sandal spread through her limbs once more.

She freed herself from the spell of the hair, put the gold sandal inside one of Strat's shirts and stumbled away.

\*     \*     \*

"The wind has brought tears to your eyes," said Dr. Lightner, handing Camilla his handkerchief.

She blotted her tears.

From Spain Camilla had sent a cable to Duffie, telling him that Strat was with Dr. Lightner's dig in Giza. Shortly she would send another cable. It would contain the news of the son's ruin. A man who stole gold from an archaeology site was destined for the hellhole of an Egyptian prison.

Hiram Stratton would have no joyful reunion. Perhaps no reunion at all. Men do not live long in such prisons, what with cholera and typhus and murder.

"See how the desert has changed, sir," she whispered. "In the dark, it stretches on like death."

"That is the very horror Pharaoh tried to fend off," agreed Dr. Lightner. "All these stones he piled into a mountain, a ladder to his eternal life, because he so feared death. That I can understand. But what possible explanation can there be for the tomb Strat found? Why did Khufu not equally prepare his mother for *her* eternal life?"

She gave back the handkerchief. Her deeds had shadowed her soul, and she was worthy of nothing, not even a square of linen.

"Miss Matthews," said Dr. Lightner, "might I ask a most special favor of you?"

"Of course, sir," she said drearily.

"The French embassy is giving a dinner party. It seems that a major American art collector is arriving in Cairo. Over the years he has purchased many a French oil painting. We are privileged to meet him and of course invite him to our excavation."

Camilla kept forgetting she was here as a reporter. Dr. Lightner would want this event in the newspapers back in America and so would the art collector. She had never read a society column in her life. She had no idea what to write about such an event.

"Miss Matthews," said Dr. Lightner, "would you do me the honor of allowing me to escort you to this dinner?"

She was not to attend as a female reporter with work to do. She had been asked as a guest. A man—a *tall* man—had sought out her company. "You are so kind, sir," she said, her words stumbling on her tongue. "I regret, however, that when I packed my trunks, I did not plan for a ball at the French embassy."

He beamed. "I have already communicated with a friend whose wife has a plentiful wardrobe and will be delighted to assist you."

Men, Camilla thought. Whoever she is, her clothing won't fit *me*. It's too late to call a dressmaker. I have literally nothing to wear on such an evening.

But she was too touched by his eagerness to tell him how silly he was; that she, Camilla Mateusz, made even dressmakers laugh. And then she remembered that Camilla Mateusz did not exist. "Dr. Lightner, it will be my privilege."

And privilege it was.

Two dressmakers used up two gowns to create one

for Camilla. With anyone else, Camilla would have been weeping. Lady Clementine made it a party.

The maids cleverly stitched an entire ten inches to the length of one gown by using the ruffles off the other. "I feel like Cinderella," said Camilla, laughing.

"Indeed," said Lady Clementine, smiling. "And here are your borrowed slippers. Silver-toed. Are they not fashionable? Luckily, my feet are large for me and your feet are small for you."

Slippers . . .

Was the gold slipper even now being discovered in Strat's trunk? Would Dr. Lightner arrive at Lady Clementine's shocked and heartsick, having learned that his cameraman was a thief? Was Strat even now in some dark prison, without light or air or hope?

What price revenge? thought Camilla. My soul. Strat's future. But I do not care about either one. I want Hiram Stratton to suffer, and he will.

"Now stand tall, my dear," said Lady Clementine. "Do not slump. Dr. Lightner is halfway in love with you, and it is your splendid height that attracts him."

"Halfway in love? With me?"

"Of course. You are as tall and strong as a pillar of Karnak, I believe he said. He is quite smitten. Of course archaeologists are a difficult group, my dear. Think twice. They are apt to be demanding, pernickety and dusty."

Camilla laughed.

"Capitalize upon your height. Throw your shoulders back. Be tall."

Nobody had ever instructed Camilla to do that.

Lady Clementine became very serious. "I see you are well educated and more than capable of presenting fine arguments during table discussions. Remember that ladies in search of a husband do not demonstrate brains." Lady Clementine fixed around Camilla's throat a beautiful necklace of shimmering pearls.

In the looking glass, Camilla found, as many a girl before her, that the wearing of beautiful clothing and jewels made her lovelier and more worthy.

"Perfect!" cried Lady Clementine. "Just so must you blush and lower your eyes. It draws men's eyes toward your bosom, you know, and away from your mind. You must not display your mind."

"Thank you," said Camilla gratefully, and they pantomimed hugs, such as decoratively dressed and coiffed women give one another.

# ANNIE

$S$ince dawn, Annie had been pointing toward the Great Pyramid. By the time Pankh arrived in mid-morning, Annie's gestures had crossed the language barrier. Renifer coaxed Pankh to take them to see the Pyramid.

Pankh was unwilling.

It took considerable pouting and pleading to change his mind. Renifer was excellent at both. Flouncing around in her dress, a very thin gauze pressed in stiff pleats, Renifer made it clear that neither gold nor gifts would make her happy. Only an excursion to the Pyramid.

Finally Pankh shrugged and nodded.

Annie held Renifer's hand as they threaded through narrow streets shaded by canvas canopies, lined with stalls selling spices and cookpots and shoes. They passed walled houses and tenements, donkeys tied in stable yards, geese in the road and even a royal procession.

Everybody knelt to gaze lovingly at a young woman on a litter covered in beaten gold. A princess, perhaps, reclining on pillows under her fringed shade? Four bulky men in tiny white kilts carried the litter on their shoulders. They walked rhythmically, one counting, like rowers on a crew team.

At the waterfront, Pankh commandeered a boat. Two men rowed half-standing, toes braced against a shelf. They moved quickly on the river, a breeze bucketing inside a much-mended sail. Annie was mesmerized by the water traffic: little boats, tubby boats, oared boats and sailboats, barges loaded with stone or casks, logs or bales.

Along the banks of the Nile, hundreds of men labored, making bricks out of mud. Villages were perched on the heights, their little mud-brick dwellings like piles of little brown wren houses.

From the Nile, they entered a canal, straight-sided as a ruler, slicing through fields and orchards, palm trees and grazing sheep. They steered into a square lake, neatly sided by cut stone, and pulled up to a wharf. Soldiers paced up and down. Small sphinxes were being set in rows.

Pankh swept his two women before him and up to a vast temple.

So modern and harsh was its design Annie felt it could have been an electric power plant in Chicago or Detroit. They did not enter the temple, but walked through a vast portico and emerged on a paved pedestrian street with awnings stretched over pillars. Flowers had been laid on the whole length of the road, bouquet after bouquet, and their feet crunched on the sun-dried petals.

At the end of the shining road was Khufu's Pyramid.

In the museum photograph, the Pyramid had been tiers of great lumps, two million brown sugar cubes, each the size of a dining room table. But at its creation, the Pyramid was slick with polished white limestone. It was surrounded by a sea of baby pyramids, flat-topped pyramids, temples, graveyards, mausoleums, steles— and one vast Sphinx, being chipped out of bedrock as Annie watched.

She began laughing with excitement. Strat must be here! This was the very place where he had taken his photographs. She must keep her eyes open.

She examined every passing man, giggling at the thought of Victorian Strat wearing a white gauze kilt like Pankh.

# RENIFER

Renifer thanked the gods for letting her live now; a time which would last for all time, embodied in this very Pyramid.

The girl of ivory was gasping in awe. Wherever she was from, she had never seen anything like this. But then, nobody had.

I was right to insist that Pankh bring us today, thought Renifer. The girl herself made it clear that this is where she must be. The reason she was put in my hands will be presented to me now.

They passed a priest in a robe of panther skins. As he approached, the priest lifted a large ostrich feather fan and hid his face behind it. Renifer was mildly surprised, because priests of the City of the Dead were the proudest men in Egypt. They did not hide their status. When she looked after him, to see which temple he entered, the priest was half-running.

They approached the burial place of Queen Hetepheres. Her chapel was a delicate structure, sitting at the foot of the thirteen-acre Pyramid like a child's toy. Over the portico, the blue and white stripes of the awning fluttered in the wind and the reflection from the silver floor was blinding.

On two blessed occasions, Renifer had been privileged to help Princess Meresankh honor her grandmother. Renifer had done the actual carrying of food to the dead queen. A royal ornament, Meresankh had never once used her hands. Handmaidens were so called because their hands did all work.

Now Renifer knelt to honor Pharaoh's mother, motioning the girl of ivory to join her. Putting their weight on one knee, they leaned forward, extending the other leg back so as to achieve a position both graceful and helpless.

Here in the shade of the awnings, the silver had not gotten too hot to touch. Reverently, Renifer kissed the floor. Here had she prayed and knelt with the queen's granddaughter. Here had she scattered droplets of sacred water and the petals of flowers.

And puddling out of the doorway onto the silver floor was something wet and red, but not sacred.

Profane.

Blood.

# IV

*Time for Sacrifice*

# RENIFER

The girl of ivory scrambled to her feet. Yanking Renifer up from her position of humility, she dragged her behind a screen of immense potted ferns just as two tomb police staggered out of the chapel. Both were bleeding heavily.

One was holding together a dreadful wound in his side, so deep it could never be sewn together; a gash from which he would die. "Pen-Meru!" he cried in a gurgling voice, and fell onto the silver pavement.

Pen-Meru? thought Renifer dizzily. But her father was not involved with the tomb police. He was a controller of the Nile, a measurer of floods and opener of canals.

The second soldier sank to his knees. Renifer thought he might live. She would tear up her dress and use it for bandages. She—

But the second soldier also whispered, "Pen-Meru."

There must be some other Pen-Meru of whom Renifer had not heard.

Pankh sprinted forward from where he had been

waiting in the shade of another temple while Renifer prayed. He pulled his dagger from its sheath.

Renifer's heart soared with pride. Pankh would be clothed in glory! For of course the tomb robbers who had done this terrible deed were inside the chapel. Brave Pankh was going to finish them off.

But Pankh did not enter the chapel. Lifting high the thin shining blade, he stabbed to death the still living tomb policeman who had sunk to his knees.

Renifer clutched the slender lotus pillar of the portico. What could this mean? How could Pankh do that? The man had been helpless! Already wounded for Pharaoh's sake.

Now Pankh was a blur, springing into the chapel itself. From within came a cry of terror. "No, Pankh! I promise—"

There was a groan and a thud.

There was silence.

The hot sickening smell of blood filled the air.

Renifer had to understand what was happening. She slipped inside the queen's chapel, careful not to block the sun, whose glint off the silver floor provided the only illumination to the interior. It took a moment to focus in the gloom. The walls were painted with scenes from the queen's life. From painted arbors hung thick purple grapes and heavy green leaves. On a ceiling of deep blue, gold stars were scattered.

Pankh stood panting in the center of the chapel. His knife stuck out of the chest of a third tomb policeman, now prostrate on the floor. In the shadows, pressed against the sacred illustrations, stood her father, Pen-Meru.

There were no other men inside the little chapel.

There was no other exit from which the killers might have fled.

No, thought Renifer. My father did not do this. Pankh did not do this. I am a slow thinker. In a moment I will understand.

She pasted herself against the wall, as if she too had been painted there.

"Good job, Pankh," said Renifer's father, grinning.

The two men slapped hands in victory and laughed. Then they frowned down upon the corpse at their feet.

"Now what?" said Pankh.

Renifer stepped forward, startling her father and her beloved, who whirled to see who was there. Father gripped a bloody dagger and Pankh tightened his fist around his own knife.

They had forgotten she existed at all, let alone that she was witness to this carnage. For one terrible moment, she thought herself in danger from the two men she loved most.

She saw now a rectangular opening in the chapel floor. Three paving stones had been lifted aside to reveal a great black shaft: the entrance to Hetepheres' tomb. It should be entirely filled with rubble—thirty feet down, all sand and rock. If the shaft was empty, then the queen's tomb had been emptied by robbers. No doubt the space below contained little of value now. The three dead policemen had walked in on the robbery.

And now her thoughts spun all too fast. Renifer felt as if she were drowning in the Nile. Mud-brown water silted up her heart. "You are tomb robbers," whispered Renifer. "It was *you* they caught."

Her father shrugged. "I have always been a tomb robber, my daughter. And your uncle with me. And Pankh."

"No! It cannot be! Father, I cannot believe it of you!"

Her father snorted. "You know perfectly well we live beyond the means of any controller of the Nile. *You* are the one yearning for gold. You and your mother insist on necklaces here and bracelets there. *You* are the ones for whom five servants are not enough; no, you must have fifteen," he snapped.

She thought of the chests of gold at home, all those jewels fit for a queen. The Sekhmet fit for a Pharaoh. Indeed. To a Pharaoh and a queen had they once belonged.

"I regret you are here, my love," said Pankh, "but since you are, you will participate."

In murder? thought Renifer. Never. She stared in loathing at their blood-flecked chests and arms.

"So far we are safe," said Pankh. "Easy lies will get us out of this. We say we are the ones who caught robbers in the act. Regrettably, they escaped, having first murdered three brave and true protectors of the queen's chapel."

Pankh and Pen-Meru laughed.

They had slain three loyal men of Pharaoh's and found it funny? Renifer felt as if she had been thrown into a sewage ditch. She could never be cleansed of the evil her father had done.

"I think, Pankh, we should say that you and I captured the actual robbers," said Pen-Meru. "They are being tortured even now, and dispatched to the Land in the West."

"What if He asks to see the prisoners?" said Pankh.

Pen-Meru shrugged. "We stake out a few peasants."

Renifer was appalled. "You would execute innocent men, pretending they robbed this tomb? But this is Egypt! Such things do not happen here."

"Would you rather that I and your future husband got staked out in the desert?" said Pen-Meru.

Renifer remembered how Pankh had stroked the goddess Sekhmet. It had not been worship, or lack of worship. It had been blackmail. *Your daughter marries me, Pen-Meru, or I bring Pharaoh into your gates to see what you have stolen from Him.*

I am the daughter of a tomb robber, thought Renifer. I will be made to marry a tomb robber. My father and husband will force my sons to be tomb robbers.

Renifer caught the distant scent of incense being burned. Somewhere a priest was obeying the sacred rites. Much good it did him, when people like her father were abroad in the land.

Here had Princess Meresankh prayed as Renifer sang, "Sky and stars make music for you. Sun and moon praise you. Gods exalt you and goddesses lift their voices." But Meresankh's grandmother was not exalted now. Renifer's family had brought her down.

Her father said to Pankh, "Even if Pharaoh believes our story, I think we will be executed. Pharaoh will find out that not only is His mother's tomb nearly empty, but her mummy is gone. He'll execute everyone in sight. He might execute the whole battalion of tomb police, even those not on duty this month."

*"You stole the queen's mummy?"* cried Renifer. Her family would be haunted forever. The powerful *ka* of the queen would waylay them by night and set traps for them by day. Renifer's children would be doomed to lives of terror.

Horror curdled in her stomach like goat's milk in the sun. She was not going to have children. She too would be staked out in the desert, three days dying, jackals waiting. Renifer's eternity would be spent in limbo, with neither rest nor joy. She hardly minded (although probably she would mind when they actually drove the stake through her). Such a fate was richly deserved by a family that profaned the tomb of a queen.

"We took the inner coffin, Renifer," said her father irritably, "because it contained the finest jewels. Of course it had her mummy in it."

"Where did you put the mummy?" said Renifer, trying not to sob. "We'll put it back. She must lie among her remaining tomb goods."

"I tossed the mummy in the desert after I peeled away the gold and silver," said Pen-Meru.

The verb he used—*toss*—was horrible in its simplicity. Children tossed balls. Her father had tossed aside the mummy of a queen as if it had no more meaning than a child's toy.

"Did you always know about this?" Renifer said in Pankh's direction. She could not face him.

"I've been helping since I was twelve." His voice was proud and even sassy, as if he had always wanted to swagger in front of her with this information, and now at last, his real self could stand before her: tomb robber.

Renifer was weeping. "Does Mother know?" she asked her father.

"She pretends not to. Like you."

"But I didn't know," she cried.

They lost interest in her silly vapors and returned to the problem at hand.

"More soldiers will be here soon," said Pen-Meru gloomily. "That means Pharaoh will be told soon. They'll go down the shaft and report to Pharaoh that not only was His mother's tomb robbed, her bones are gone. We are dead men."

"I've got it," said Pankh excitedly. "We tell Him that we, in our glory, prevented the robbery. The valor of Pen-Meru and his future son-in-law, Pankh, led to the deaths of some robbers—but the others fled. We tell Pharaoh that since the escaped evildoers now know where the opening of the queen's tomb is, we recommend an immediate solution to Pharaoh."

Pankh was almost jumping up and down in his delight. Renifer wondered how she had ever found this man attractive.

"You will recall, Pen-Meru," said her beloved, "that adjacent to that temple being constructed close to the Pyramid is an unused tomb. It was built for Princess Nitiqret of Blessed Memory, but she chose to be buried in her husband's tomb. How we will praise the vacant tomb! We will convince Pharaoh that it is fit for the *ka* of His mother. Even now, we will explain to Him, we are swiftly removing the tomb furniture from this defiled spot and have taken the blessed body of Hetepheres to its new and safe resting place." He folded his arms over his chest, swollen with pride at his brilliant idea.

"It's not much of a tomb," said Pen-Meru doubtfully. "It's hardly a closet. They sank it very deep, but since Nitiqret was buried elsewhere, they never began the wall paintings or finished up—"

"Who cares?" said Pankh impatiently. "Pharaoh is never going to descend the shaft to see. He will believe you. You in your radiance will have acted swiftly and with reverence to rescue a queen whose safe harbor has been invaded. I will treat you as a god before Him, marveling in the splendor of your quick thinking and willingness to die for the queen. He'll fall for it."

"Maybe," said Renifer's father. "But maybe not. Pharaoh isn't stupid."

"May I remind you what will happen if we allow Pharaoh's servants to climb down that shaft?"

And then the time for planning was over. The chapel filled with more tomb police. Shocked and saddened by the loss of their colleagues, they let Pen-Meru take charge. He motioned them into a huddle, giving instructions.

"We work quickly to transfer the remaining tomb furniture," said Pen-Meru. "Pharaoh will kill every one of us for failing to keep His mother's tomb safe. But if He thinks that in the end, we *did* keep her safe . . . Well, then. Not only do we survive, He will pay us each a great reward."

The tomb police, afraid of the wrath of Pharaoh, agreed.

Renifer felt there was a flaw in the plan. Everybody knew where tomb entrances were. The moment a chapel was raised, the world understood that the tomb lay beneath.

Does Pharaoh think nobody knows where He will lie? wondered Renifer. Having built the largest pyramid in the world above His shaft? Not that anybody could ever shift those stones. Still . . .

For the first time she realized that *Pharaoh would not bury Himself beneath His Pyramid.* He would have a real grave site, hidden and safe. The Pyramid was many things, and one was trickery.

Every tomb policeman went to work immediately. They delegated and planned, summoning laborers and torches, planks and ropes, carts and baskets.

Although Hetepheres' sarcophagus weighed many tons, removing it was not difficult, as the equipment was close at hand and used every day. Once lifted up, it was placed on rollers, hitched to ropes that were hitched to men, and moved to the mouth of the new tomb.

Nitiqret's shaft was far deeper. Affixing the strongest of papyrus ropes, the men lowered the sarcophagus easily, their only worry that the ropes would split under the weight and the coffin drop to the bottom and break into a thousand pieces. But that did not happen.

The remaining pieces of tomb furniture—only a bed canopy and a carrying chair had not been stolen—were taken down and piled against the wall. The gold hieroglyphs of the queen's name glittered against the black ebony of her bed.

"Now," said Pen-Meru, "we go to Pharaoh."

Renifer did not want to imagine the scene with Pharaoh, as her father and her future husband outdid themselves with lies to the Living God. If Pharaoh believed the untruths Pen-Meru put before Him, would it prove that He was man and not God? And if He were man, and not God, what then was Egypt? What were the sun and the Nile? Who controlled them and made them great?

Renifer felt bludgeoned by the heat and sun, the shock and shame.

"The more distinguished the ceremony of reburying Hetepheres," said Pankh, "the less Pharaoh will question the details. Girls are useful in ceremonies. They add a feeling of reverence and grace. You, Renifer, will sing. He loves your voice. And the girl of ivory we will dress as a handmaiden. She is just the kind of gift to please Pharaoh."

Renifer had forgotten the girl of ivory.

Was she indeed a *ka*? Could she be Queen Hetepheres' *ka*? Once Father had thrown Hetepheres' body to the jackals, had the *ka* lost its way in the papyrus swamp? Or could the girl of ivory be a messenger sent by Hetepheres?

Why had Pankh cried out the name of the queen when he first saw the girl of ivory? Because he knew what he had done to Hetepheres? Or because her *ka* put those syllables in his mouth?

Renifer found the girl still in the shade of the silver portico among the fronds of the green ferns. She seemed neither afraid nor confused, but lightly embraced Renifer, as if to say that she understood.

The great sun was sinking now in bloodred splendor. Pharaoh's barge was visible in the square lagoon far down the causeway.

"The timing is good," said Pankh. "Tomorrow Pharaoh has planned a great feast to welcome the return of the admiral from Lebanon. Not only did the admiral successfully acquire twelve ships of cedar logs, he brought dancing bears and trained dwarfs. Pharaoh will want to complete the reburial tonight, so that tomorrow He can concentrate on the celebrations."

Renifer was beginning to believe the outrageous plan might succeed.

Her father said, "You, Renifer, will utter the sacraments when we seal His mother in darkness. You will describe how the girl of ivory arrived; how she was sent by a *ka*. Pharaoh loves omens from the next world. Don't say she's just a foreigner who needed a bath. Then, deep in the night, we bring Him to the top of the

131

new shaft. We let Pharaoh catch a glimpse of gold at the bottom, shining in the moonlight. He will assume that everything originally with the queen is still with the queen! And because we left behind her stone sarcophagus—after all, it has no resale value—He will think her silver and gold coffin is within."

"What do you bet," said Pankh, "that in His gratitude, He even invites us to the feast for the admiral?"

Pen-Meru laughed and bet the golden Sekhmet. Pankh bet six gold necklaces. They slapped hands to seal the bet.

Farmers were yanked from a field. They insisted they were not tomb robbers. But of course, that is what a robber would shout as he was carried to the desert edge. Once they understood their fate, they began screaming and fighting, but to no avail. The stakes were driven in slowly, to prolong the pain.

Renifer felt the stakes through her own heart; through all her hopes.

"What if the girl of ivory runs away or behaves badly?" asked Father.

"She loves gold," said Pankh. "Adorn her in much gold and she will be happy."

# CAMILLA

O h! the compliments of the men as they gathered for dinner at the French embassy in Cairo. The smiles with which the men greeted Camilla, upon being introduced. The admiring eyes. The tender remarks. Dizzy with excitement, Camilla flirted and laughed.

"If only we were not going to war!" cried the British officers. "We would surely beg the pleasure of your company at our dances, Miss Matthews."

How splendid the British were, chests crossed by sashes, hung with bejeweled military crosses, decked out in many-colored ribbons.

Dr. Lightner bowed to them, saying with great courtesy, "I hope you will join us for a dance I will give in her honor."

"But of course!" cried the guests. "Such a beautiful woman deserves everything in her honor."

"Ah," said the French, sounding so intimate that Camilla blushed, *"quelle perfection."*

Camilla could not stop smiling. Neither could Dr. Lightner. Camilla could have swirled around the room forever, height forgotten, as she and Dr. Lightner drifted from group to group.

"What a pleasure this is," said Dr. Lightner, as they waltzed in graceful circles. "Normally I am the outcast. The tedious scholar who writes books. Tonight, I have grace and appeal, Miss Matthews, because of your company."

Her very height prevented even Dr. Lightner from knowing how young she was; it was a disguise in inches. She was by far the youngest at the party, but she was holding her own. She wanted the introductions to go on forever, but of course, eventually the guest of honor arrived and they must all sit down for a formal dinner.

The guest of honor was very fat, strapped into his dinner jacket and cummerbund. His jowls layered down onto his chest and his arms were so thick he could hardly bend at the elbows.

"A very rich man indeed," said a British officer, admiring the amount of meat and brandy it took to achieve such girth.

"Excellent mustache," said another.

The guest had a strong American accent. The British flinched slightly at his vulgar words and the French raised their eyebrows. The Germans could not be bothered to cross the room. But Dr. Lightner was most eager to meet the gentleman. "An American art collector!" he whispered. "It's very new. All the best people are doing it now. It gives one hope for America. We will bring him to the excavation."

And then for the first time that evening, Dr. Lightner's face drooped into tired lines. "He will expect glory," said the archaeologist sadly, "and find only potsherds. He will expect gold. I did not want to sully this lovely evening, Miss Matthews, with the sad fact of what happened this afternoon. We cannot find the gold sandal."

Camilla was so flushed with excitement that another layer of pink in her cheeks was not noticeable. "It must have been mislaid," she said.

"Nobody mislays gold. They do, however, steal it."

"No!" cried Camilla. "Surely not. Who at your dig would stoop so low?" She wondered when they would search the gentlemen's tent. They might not, now that she thought of it. It would be too great an insult for young men so full of importance.

"Hush," murmured Dr. Lightner. "Let us not speak of regrettable events during this fine occasion. Come, it is our turn to be presented to the guest of honor."

Camilla was oddly afraid. This close, the body did not seem grand, but gross. The mustache not lush, but graying moss creeping over the lips and into the mouth. The swollen hand that gripped hers was girded in rings so tight that the flesh burst out around them. The man's breath stank of pipe tobacco and he had already had too much brandy.

The party felt infected.

"And this lovely lady?" he said. A smile crawled out from behind the moss of his mustache.

Camilla tried to smile, but did not achieve it.

"This," said Archibald Lightner proudly, "is my guest, sir. Miss Camilla Matthews."

A flicker of amusement went through the man's eyes, and Camilla felt owned, as a slave might be, or a factory hand.

"Ah, yes," said the guest of honor. "The famous Miss Matthews. The reporter from Kansas."

In all America, only Mr. Duffie knew there was a Camilla Matthews who claimed to be a reporter. Mr. Duffie and one other man. Camilla tried to step back, but the man did not release his grip, as a gentleman should. "Hiram Stratton, Sr., at your service, ma'am," said he.

Camilla tried to extricate her hands from his paws but he did not allow it. She would have to scrub her fingers as she had scrubbed herself from the dread of leprosy.

I would rather have leprosy than touch Hiram Stratton, she thought. Why did I not realize that he would come? It is my own telegraph that brought him. Of course he would not trust me to bring his beloved son home. After all, I had no intention of doing it. I intended his son to live out his days, or at least a few years, in an Egyptian prison.

But I have failed.

Whether or not the gold sandal is found among Strat's belongings, nothing will happen to the boy. Hiram Stratton's power is tangible even in this room that belongs to another government. His power will work anywhere. In Egypt, being paid off has been a tradition for thousands of years. There will still be a joyful reunion, and father and son will go home to burn down yet another factory.

"Mr. Stratton, sir!" cried Dr. Lightner. "What a privilege to encounter a man of your stature. It is my hope to be permitted to bring you to Giza, that I may myself escort you among the ancient Egyptian monuments, and have the great pleasure of showing you the excavation under my supervision. Just this week, we uncovered a hitherto unknown tomb. It is full of mystery."

"Fine, fine," said Hiram Stratton, already bored.

"In fact, my good sir," said Dr. Lightner, now somewhat uneasy, "among the young men spending a year with me in lieu of being broadened by travel in the more usual places, young men educated at Harvard and Yale, Princeton and Dartmouth . . ." Dr. Lightner paused, as if hoping he need not go on.

"Among those young men," said Hiram Stratton, "is my own son. Do not be uncomfortable with the admission. It is I who am ashamed. He went to Yale, but did not succeed. He has not, in fact, succeeded anywhere. He lacks capacity for anything except failure."

The French were horrified that a father would speak like that. The British were expressionless. The Germans, of course, had still not bothered to cross the room.

"I've come to bring him home," said Hiram Stratton. "He belongs in prison and I plan to put him there." The man's face split open in what must have been a smile. Camilla could not look at it.

"In prison?" repeated Dr. Lightner, appalled. "Surely not, Mr. Stratton. He seems a delightful fellow. Has taken fine pictures. In fact, he's the one who found the tomb about which I am so excited!"

"I was not blessed with a good son," said Hiram Stratton. "Throughout his life it has been necessary to curb him. I incarcerated him in an asylum for the good of the community."

You did not! thought Camilla. You locked him up because he defied you. It was easy to show the factory workers who was boss: burn their jobs. It was easy to show your son, too. Whip Strat until he cringed in the manner you like to see in dogs.

"He escaped," said Hiram Stratton. "Attacked the staff and vanished. Not only that, he kidnapped two innocent children."

He did not! They were not children. They went with him joyfully. He was saving them. Their own families do not want them back!

"I have come here," said Hiram Stratton, "to see Egypt, of course. To admire your excavation, of course. To consider a major donation. But alas, to administer a lasting punishment to my son." He did not mean that word alas. He gloated.

Camilla had thought that Duffie's lies were about the nature of St. Rafael's patients; Duffie feared she would not agree to get near leprosy. How terribly wrong she had been. His lies were about the reason for locating the son. Camilla had not been sent to arrange a joyful reunion. She had been sent so that the father could ruin his own boy.

Camilla had chosen not to believe Katie's version of Strat's character. But Katie, who knew so much of cruelty, had singled Strat out as a true and decent friend.

Why did I not believe Katie? thought Camilla.

Far from ruining Hiram Stratton, she had played into his hands. Not simply locating the boy, but putting the boy into an immensely worse situation. Whatever lies and fabrications Mr. Stratton brought from America, it would be no lie that the missing gold sandal was in Strat's possession; that Strat had dishonored the entire dig; that he was a thief.

"He was also," said the French attaché thoughtfully, "involved in some way in the death of those two young men who fell from the Pyramid."

"No, no," said Dr. Lightner, "we've been through that, he was in no way involved except that I instructed him to deliver the bodies to you."

"Since he is a kidnapper," said Hiram Stratton, "it would not surprise me if he were also a murderer. It is for trial that I bring him back to New York. I spawned a criminal and as a criminal he will be treated."

The man is happy, thought Camilla. He looks forward to throwing his own child to the jackals. He rejoices at the thought of his son suffering.

Why? Because the son is beautiful while he is gross? Because the son is kind while he believes in cruelty? Or because Hiram Stratton, Sr., is truly evil?

Hiram Stratton could not be allowed to continue. Such verbiage would simply ruin the festivities. Lady

Clementine and the ambassador's wife bustled about, tugging here and there to line the guests up for their entry into the dining room.

"My dear Miss Matthews," said the French ambassador.

I am not evil, thought Camilla, but I am in its neighborhood. Having placed young Stratton in jeopardy, I must now save him. The sandal, in fact, is minor. Kidnapping and assault are not. I cannot let his father have him.

She smiled at the French ambassador, who said, "Might I escort you to the dinner table, my dear, where if you will be so kind, I will seat you next to our guest of honor."

Camilla's bare arm rubbed against the sleeve of Hiram Stratton's dinner jacket. Her left hand brushed his when she picked up a fork and he a spoon.

She was unable to eat, but in a world where fainting delicate women were prized, failure to eat was much admired. She was unable to speak, but in a world where only the words of men had value, a quiet woman was a jewel.

"My dear Miss Matthews," said Hiram Stratton, "I detest a woman who babbles and you, dear girl, have a great capacity for silence. What a pleasure. I have never permitted one of my wives to chatter."

"*One* of your wives, sir?"

"I am in the midst of divorcing my fourth."

It was an admission so outrageous, Camilla could not believe he had said it in public. Even to use the word divorce at an elegant gathering like this was vulgar. She trembled at the suffering of those four women, sharing a life and a bed with this monster. "I assume your fourth wife babbled," she said.

"Precisely." Hiram Stratton laughed hugely and spilled red wine. "*And* demanded *and* whined *and* argued. A man cannot be expected to put up with that."

"Of course not," said Camilla.

"Miss Matthews," said Hiram Stratton very softly, "you are a fine detective. Nothing escapes you, does it? You should know, my dear, that nothing escapes me either."

Their eyes met. What could he mean? Had he already discerned that she was making plans for Strat's escape?

Hidden by the starched white damask tablecloth, the man had the gall to put his hand on her knee. He began to inch her skirt upward, in order to touch her bare skin.

Camilla's choices were few. To stab him with her fork would be a breach of manners. How would the French feel then about Dr. Lightner, bringing so uncouth a creature to their party? Lady Clementine would take back her dress and her pearls, knowing Camilla had not the grace to handle situations like a lady.

Yet she could not allow it to happen.

It dawned on her that this was what Hiram Stratton referred to. He had noticed Camilla and she belonged to him, having accepted his false letter of introduction and his money, and he would take her in other ways as well.

Camilla could not think clearly. Failure to think clearly had happened to at least four other women in the presence of Hiram Stratton, Sr. She looked desperately at Lady Clementine and found she had underestimated this fine person. Lady Clementine tapped her silver knife gently against a crystal glass, and a sweet note rang out through the room. The ladies stood, and quickly the men rose with them.

Hiram Stratton struggled to join them, his bulk and the difficult position into which he had maneuvered his hands slowing him down.

"Gentlemen," said the ambassador's wife graciously, "we leave you to your dessert and brandy, so your conversations may turn to war and politics, while we retire to the garden, and our conversations turn to fashion and weddings."

A servant pulled Camilla's chair out for her and the gentlemen bade the ladies *au revoir.* Hiram Stratton said into Camilla's ear, "Do not forget that you are my employee. You will do all that you are told." A smirk lay behind his moss mustache. *"All."*

# ANNIE

Annie was very impressed by the clothing placed on her body.

A shift of fine linen hung straight from shoulder to ankle. Over that was placed an entire dress of linked beads, gold and blue and a rich dark red, laced into a thousand one-inch squares. When she moved, the beads rearranged themselves in a chorus of clicks.

Renifer's servant painted Annie's eyes far into her hairline, and into her hair worked a garland of shiny green leaves and bright flowers. On her feet were placed gold sandals, which glowed as if they contained the sun and eternity itself. Annie had never seen workmanship so beautiful, so impossible.

Of course, she might as well have been wearing lead slabs. She did not see how she was going to walk, but it turned out that walking didn't matter. She and Renifer were lifted like dolls into a double sedan chair, placed gently on soft pillows and carried on the shoulders of men whose muscles bulged as they strained.

The streets of Memphis were quiet. It was very late.

Most torches had been put out; most music had ended; most people slept.

All afternoon and all evening, Annie had thought about the three dead men, killed, it seemed, by Pankh and Pen-Meru.

There had been police, full of questions; their uniforms and weapons different from police in her time, but their demeanor and posture the same.

With so much coming and going among guards and so much confusion as they shifted things from one tomb to another, Annie could have vanished into the vast acreage of tombs and blocky mausoleums. But Time had surely given her into Renifer's hands for a purpose. It had to be Strat. And yet there had been no sign of him.

It was not fair. She had expected to find Strat. To love and be loved once more. Strat must be above her in time, pushing a trowel into the very sand on which she stood. Annie felt betrayed and angry. She wanted to yell at somebody, but nobody shared her language. She had tried to comfort Renifer when the girl wept over the farmers plucked from the fields like chicken for dinner.

But Renifer had sunk into a silent despair and nothing brought her out of it.

When they were dressed by the maids, Renifer refused every single piece of gold and jewelry.

Pankh and Pen-Meru were at the door constantly, demanding speed.

The maids were frightened. Annie tried to keep her own composure, but it was difficult, understanding so little of the events, and feeling so very sorry for Renifer, in love with a man who made a habit of stabbing police-men to death.

She and Renifer sat shoulder to shoulder in the litter, Annie's beads making dents in both of them. At last Renifer roused herself. She took Annie's first finger and pressed it against Annie's lips, shaking her head twice: *No.* Then she pressed her own finger against Annie's lips and raised her eyebrows.

She was requesting silence. Annie smiled and nodded agreement, rather proud to be communicating so clearly. With her thumbs, Renifer flattened the edges of Annie's smile away. Again she shook her head.

Whatever they were about to do, it was no laughing matter.

Oh, Strat! thought Annie. What is going to happen? Why aren't you here?

They were carried to the river and aboard the same barge that had been at the Pyramid lagoon that morning. Trimmed in gold, fluttering with flags and bright with paint, it was fit for a king. Along its deck, soldiers swung spears whose shafts were encircled with gold.

Not king, thought Annie. *Pharaoh.*

Khufu himself.

She was to be in the presence of the most powerful man on this earth? When she could not understand what anybody said? When she had seen how readily they murdered people here?

In front of his feet, as in front of the queen's chapel, the deck was silver. In the torchlight, it possessed a mys-terious flickering gleam.

She and Renifer were lifted out of the sedan chair, while Pen-Meru and Pankh stepped ahead to kneel. They knelt in the awkward gymnast's perch that Renifer had used, one leg extended behind, other knee touching the floor, forehead pressed against the silver. In such a position, a man was helpless. If an order were given to have them killed, how simple it would be.

Fear was palpable. In their anxiety, people breathed so deeply it almost caused the sails to billow forth.

Annie suddenly realized the men were kneeling to Pharaoh. His throne was so immense, so high, and he so utterly still that she had not seen him. He did not seem to breathe at all. Wrapped against the evening chill in a magnificent cape of leopard skin, a towering crown upon his head, he did not appear to notice the humans at his feet. He did not even seem real.

Perhaps he's a mummy, thought Annie. Perhaps they worship a dead man.

But Pharaoh was very much alive, and very angry.

Whatever Renifer's father said infuriated the king. In one hand was a staff that he pounded against the deck of the ship, and in the other a short whip, which he flailed through the air, causing men to fling themselves flat on the deck.

Renifer was trembling badly. Annie tried to stave off her own fears. Much as she wanted Strat, she hoped he was not here. There was too much danger.

The barge left the wharf and moved slowly on the river, rowed by men sitting below the deck. Annie watched the rising and falling tips of the oars and heard the gentle slap as they entered the Nile.

Abruptly Pharaoh waved Pen-Meru to silence. Pen-Meru dashed his forehead on the deck and Pharaoh stood up. He barked short syllables, angry and quick. Renifer whimpered, and then guided Annie forward. It was almost impossible to move in the beaded dress and the inflexible gold sandals. Renifer positioned Annie in front of Pharaoh, running a hand up Annie's spine to keep her standing, while she herself knelt.

Pharaoh stared at Annie. He seemed made of wood. His eyes blinked slowly and thickly, as if fastened to hinges rarely used.

Courtiers reverently removed the great crown, placing it upon a pedestal designed to hold that amazing headgear. Pharaoh swung the great cape off his shoulders. He was bare-chested except for a medallion encrusted with jewels, and his muscular body was scarred from some danger he had survived. Claw scrapes, perhaps, from the very leopard whose skin he now wore.

This man, thought Annie, would skin anybody if he felt like it.

But it was Annie whose skin interested Pharaoh.

She tried to breathe as infrequently as he did. To show this man her fear would be a grave error. Not one man or woman on this barge had dared look Pharaoh in the eye. Annie stared right at him. For a moment, their gazes locked: a king and a blue-eyed trespasser from another time.

Her stomach churned. The slabs of gold on her feet seemed to drag her down.

Pharaoh seemed almost to smile, and the smile was one she had seen before. Where? On what face? Because she had certainly never seen his.

The barge arrived at the square lake and the harsh temple. Far down the torchlit causeway loomed his Pyramid, stunning and graceful by night.

Annie and Renifer were lifted once more into their sedan chair, while Pharaoh was placed on a similar, but immensely larger, chair. It took eight men to lift him.

A procession was formed.

Annie had thought Pharaoh would be attended by a cast of thousands. But only a dozen soldiers and a few priests accompanied the king.

They passed through the portals of the stern temple and under the banners of its pillars. They walked with measured pace along the causeway. They passed the chapel where the murders had happened. Renifer held tight to Annie. Her hand felt as thin and cold as bones.

Instead of lighting more torches for more light, the priests doused torches for *less* light.

What dark ceremony, what dark thoughts were soon to be expressed? What dark deeds?

They stopped at the shaft down which Pen-Meru and Pankh and their cohorts had lowered the sarcophagus. Annie and Renifer were lifted from their conveyance and brought to stand next to Pharaoh at the opening in the earth.

The priests chanted, and rocked on their heels, and

anointed surfaces with oil from holy vessels. Renifer sang. What a beautiful soprano she had! The notes soared among the tombs and the dead, echoing off a million stones.

Pharaoh closed his eyes in prayer.

Annie prayed to Time. *Take me to Strat.*

She could hear Time laughing, and turned quickly, but it was Pankh.

# RENIFER

Renifer stood with her head bowed and her eyes fixed on her painted toes. She knew now why her father smirked at power. Power was held by those who told the best lies.

For Pharaoh had believed Pen-Meru. He accepted Pankh's lies. Renifer stood in shame as deep as the mud in which peasants toiled.

If Pharaoh did not understand, and she did, was it Renifer's duty to speak the truth? Should she crush Him with the knowledge that His mother's bones were scattered and dishonored?

Pharaoh, God Himself, must bring order to the chaos of living. His power caused the Nile to rise, bringing the water that grew the grain that baked the bread that kept Egypt alive. To upset Pharaoh was to ruin the lives of all. Therefore silence was best.

Or was it?

One priest anointed the site with sacred oils while another burned incense. An acolyte set down a freshly killed duck and a basket of dates.

O Hetepheres! Your interment should include a train

of priestesses! Paid musicians and a choir. A parade and seventy days of feasting. Petals of roses strewn for hundreds of yards and fine perfumes distributed among thousands of mourners.

"It's a hundred feet down the shaft, Great King," said Pen-Meru, gleeful with success. "Infinitely more secure than the previous tomb. All was accomplished with speed but sacred dignity. Those laborers who moved her tomb goods have been sent West."

Renifer was sick. So every worker her father had commanded this afternoon had been executed. Oh, the foul deaths for which her father was responsible!

I cannot atone, thought Renifer. No matter what parts of this ritual I do, it will mean nothing.

She washed her face and hands with holy drops and sang to the Nile, because the river was Egypt and Egypt was the river.

When Pharaoh had added His blessing, He said, "The priestess of ivory does not sing?"

"She has no language, sire," said Renifer.

Seven times, she stepped forward and then backward to sanctify the shaft. Kissing each one, she placed before the new tomb four amulets: cat, scarab, cow and ibis. From a spun-glass goblet of holy water, Renifer sipped first, and then gave each person present a taste of the holy water. Even the girl of ivory.

The ritual was complete.

Pharaoh stepped up to the hole and gazed steadily down the open shaft.

Nobody dared speak. Perhaps the God was praying in

His heart. Or perhaps He had some plan of which He had not yet spoken.

"In very ancient times," said the Living God slowly, "a queen was buried with her living servants. I sometimes wonder if it is sufficiently reverent to allow dolls to represent those servants."

The hundreds of dolls which represented palace staff had of course been stolen early on. They were easy to sell. Well-to-do people needed them for their own burials and never asked when the dolls had been made or for whom.

Pharaoh flicked a wrist and two of His palace guards stepped forward. They carried between them a long open box, whose weight caused their muscles to bulge and quiver with effort. It contained gold. Necklaces were draped over tiaras, earrings tumbled through armpieces, bracelets tangled among pectorals.

Pankh and Pen-Meru gasped. Only Renifer knew that it was not with reverence. It was with greed.

"For the most part," said Pharaoh, "I agree with the new theory of symbolism. For the most part, I agree that when the queen my mother is given eternal life, her servants will arise to wait upon her. But the queen my mother has been wrenched from the resting place she herself prepared."

"It is so," spoke the listeners, because agreeing with a king was always correct. It was not permitted to look into Pharaoh's eyes, but that was easy, because their eyes were fastened on all that gold.

"The beautiful silent priestess, the color of ivory," said Pharaoh, "will be perfect."

Pen-Meru nodded.

Pankh nodded.

The soldiers, the priest and his acolyte nodded.

Renifer nodded. Ancient custom might erase some of what her family had done. Only the whitest bulls and cows were sacrificed, and was this not the whitest of females? Had not Renifer's own nurse seen from the first that the girl was intended for sacrifice?

The girl of ivory was not aware of their survey, nor had she any way of knowing what Pharaoh had just decreed: that she was to serve Hetepheres for eternity. She was staring at Pharaoh's Pyramid as if she could not believe that she stood beside it.

Soon, thought Renifer, you will stand below it.

It was imperative that the girl should neither scream nor fight. She must not understand what was happening. Normally she would have been given a special drink to prepare her body, but none was prepared for this event. Renifer wondered how to be sure that the girl participated graciously and fully.

An extraordinary thing occurred. Pharaoh Himself began to clothe her in the gold he had brought along. Around her neck He fastened a gold pectoral of spread wings, which not only covered her throat but fell almost to her waist. He Himself adjusted the weight behind her neck to keep the pectoral at the right height. One by one, He slid gleaming bracelets over her wrist and past the curve of her elbow, until her arms were solid with gold.

When He was done, the girl could scarcely have moved, so weighted was she now by gold. And such was the glory of gold that the girl was hypnotized by it. They needed no specially prepared drink to control her behavior. Wearing the gold was her drug.

It is good, thought Renifer. Her heart eased, knowing that the queen had this lovely servant for eternity.

Pharaoh studied the awesome triangle of His Pyramid. When at last He spoke, His voice seemed directed to the stars in the sky. "Such a perfect sacrifice," He said finally, "must have an escort into the tomb."

Pankh and Pen-Meru stiffened with panic. If Pharaoh designated a priest to go down the shaft, the priest would see there were hardly any tomb furnishings; that the seal on the sarcophagus was brand new and the tomb pitifully small for a queen. He would bellow the news, Pharaoh Himself might descend, and all would be executed after all.

"It worries me a little," said Pharaoh, "that the girl of ivory might cry out and defile the moment of her sacrifice."

There was sand and dust and the cold wind of night.

Renifer with her bare shoulders shivered.

Pharaoh looked into her eyes and she tried to keep her eyes on the ground where they belonged, but her eyes were caught on His and she could not even blink.

"Perhaps, my little singer of song," said Khufu, his smile broad and kingly, "you would lead the sacrifice into the tomb. With you by her side, she will be smiling."

Renifer listened to the faint lap of water from the lagoon, the distant voices of the crew on the barge. Khufu was asking her to travel down into the tomb. He was not suggesting that she would ever travel back out of it.

Her father said, "What an honor for my daughter, Great King."

Her once beloved said, "What an honor for my bride, Great King."

Wind whistled through stones stacked for future tombs.

"Will you, little singer of song, do me this honor?" asked Pharaoh.

As if Renifer had a choice. As if she were permitted to say, "No, thank you," and go home to her mother.

To the Lord of the Two Lands, Renifer said, "I will."

# ANNIE

Annie did not see how they were all going to descend into Hetepheres' tomb. Especially her. With all this gold she probably weighed as much as the Statue of Liberty.

Renifer was lowered first, in a basket, like some scary ride at an amusement park. Annie was clearly next, then Pharaoh himself. Renifer held a torch in her hand but Annie was not given one. Renifer was lowered gently and without any bumping or lurching. Annie swallowed nervously and went down after her.

Pharaoh said something, his thin smile flickering like a flame or a snake's tongue.

That's who he reminds me of, she thought. A viper.

She was relieved when her basket fell below the level of the earth and beyond the power of his eyes. The shaft was very steep. She touched gouges in the stone, toeholds, perhaps for those without ropes or baskets.

At the bottom of the shaft, yet more gold glittered in the light of Renifer's torch.

Where do they get all this gold? she thought. Is Egypt

full of gold mines? Or do they send pirates abroad, to loot and pillage?

At the bottom, she was surprised and disappointed. It was just a small stone room. Nothing there except the few pieces shifted from the other tomb. The vast sarcophagus, the bed canopy, the sedan chair. The gold she had seen from higher up was just one tray, far less than she had on her own body.

Well, it sure isn't Tutankhamen's tomb, she thought. But probably this is just the outer room. Once we start exploring, we'll see the better rooms.

She wondered what ceremonies would take place underground.

She could hear Pharaoh being lowered, his basket not coming down quite so lightly as her own, for it seemed to smack the walls. She looked toward the shaft, but the feet of Pharaoh did not appear. A great slab was being lowered on ropes. Renifer's torchlight showed it to be no beautiful painted object. Just rock.

Annie could make no sense of it.

When the huge stone had settled onto the bottom, the person above let go of the ropes. They fell into a coil of their own. Were she and Renifer meant to do something with those ropes?

A second stone was lowered onto the ropes from the first stone. Together, the two stones sealed the shaft. There was no longer an opening. Nobody else could come down.

Nobody could go back up, either.

A terrible racket began. It took Annie several moments to realize that rocks were being dropped down the shaft. Rocks that hit and ricocheted and echoed. Filling the shaft. Filling it for eternity.

Annie and Renifer were being buried alive.

# V

*Time for Ghosts*

# STRAT

Strat was sitting about ten courses up the Pyramid, feet dangling, head resting in the corner made by two huge stones. Across the Giza plateau, by carriage and sedan chair, by donkey and camel came the party guests, having spent the night in Cairo, and only now returning to the dig.

Miss Matthews and Dr. Lightner were astride donkeys so small their feet dragged in the dust. Strat hoped Miss Matthews had enjoyed herself. In his youth, he had been to many parties and enjoyed them. But he was nineteen now and felt no desire to attend more. The girl whose company had made him happy had been lost.

He was touched to see the stern Archibald Lightner so smitten. It was in part Miss Matthews' height: Dr. Lightner need not stoop to deal with her, as if she were a child. It was in part her independence. Elderly British ladies traveled alone all the time (although of course with a maid and a companion). But Miss Matthews had come truly alone, not even a maid. Strat tried to imagine a father or brother permitting her to be a reporter at all, let alone voyage by herself to a place quite primitive.

Laughing, Dr. Lightner and Miss Matthews dismounted easily, since they were taller than their rides, and walked the last quarter mile holding hands. Strat wanted to embrace them both in his joy for them.

He could hardly wait to tell the archaeologist about his latest discovery.

When the great man had left yesterday evening for Cairo, the entire camp had been distressed by the missing gold sandal. All spirits had sunk. Had the only true treasure in the tomb waited thousands of years—only to be stolen in 1899?

This morning, Dr. Lightner's college assistants had decided to search every tent and trunk, but Strat, unwilling to trespass upon the belongings of others, continued his own investigation. He had convinced himself that if *one* pile of rock turned out to be plaster hiding a tomb entrance, *another* pile of rock would surely turn out to be plaster, and hiding a tomb entrance.

Since dawn, he had been walking about with a small ball peen hammer, swinging it against rocks, hoping each time for a sifting of plaster. A hour ago, such an event had occurred.

Strat put up no flag to mark the location, but he knew exactly where it was. If he paced parallel to the causeway precisely forty-six steps, heel pressed against toe, from Hetepheres' shaft, he would see the tiny white smash mark of his hammer on a long flat thin stone.

A surprisingly large group was returning with Dr. Lightner. Clearly he intended to show off his excavation to many who had attended the French party. Strat hoped the gold sandal had been located by now, as it was sure to impress the visitors.

He recognized two German scholars from a dig in Saqqara; two Italians who wished to study Dr. Lightner's finds; a handful of British army officers; the hieroglyphic expert; and even the French military attaché.

Finally, in a small open carriage pulled by two straining donkeys, their keeper hitting them continually with sticks lest they give up and fall down, rode a very heavy man, all belly and jowls, with a dusty wrinkled hide like a rhinoceros.

No, thought Strat. It cannot be.

He closed his eyes for a moment, and tried again. The image did not change.

It was good that he wasn't at the top of the Pyramid, Strat thought, or he would have followed the example of the two young Frenchmen, and just rolled off. Arriving dead at the bottom would be better than encountering his father.

Father was a word that should be precious, redolent of respect and honor; of example and pride. This was not the case for Strat.

What mattered to his father were investments. All life was an investment: a servant, a wife, a factory, a dinner party. All investments must pay off or be discarded. At no time would a losing investment be kept . . . even if that investment were his only son.

Chained up in the asylum, Strat had promised God that if he ever got out, he would not follow his father's example. Rather, he would help others. Much harder, he would accept help, and not arrogantly insist that he could stand alone.

But it was Katie who had fulfilled those promises. She was help even to lepers beneath the feet of the Lord. And her greatest gift, the one that dazzled and shamed him, came when Katie chose to say good-bye, so Strat might have a life unencumbered by a deformed girl he could not forever pretend was his sister.

I have helped nobody, he thought now. I have leaped into adventure and thrown away my promise. And the Lord knows exactly how I have behaved.

Dizzily, Strat stared at Hiram Stratton clambering out of the carriage. Now Father stood inside Strat's new life; touched Strat's tent and cot; spoke to Strat's friends and colleagues.

How could Hiram Stratton, Sr., have located Strat? And why would he care enough to travel all the way to Egypt? His father loathed exercise and particularly loathed hot weather. What could he be doing here? Such a man might have anything in mind, but not anything good.

A commotion sprang up among the tents, of course. His father could not bear peace or calm. He must have action and argument. He must provoke and antagonize, because destroying the serenity of others demonstrated power. Nobody, not anywhere on this earth, not even in the desert, could hide from the personality of Hiram Stratton, Sr.

From this distance Strat was indistinguishable from the hordes of tourists, both European and Egyptian, climbing and picnicking on the rugged edges of Khufu's Pyramid. In a trice, Strat could mingle with the crowd below; buy from a vendor a robe of the sort worn by local men. He could wind around his head a turban and then hire a camel. He could vanish up the Nile, as British troops were vanishing into the misty unknown of darkest Africa.

This time he would be sufficiently intelligent to use another name.

Strat slipped down from his perch. What name to use? Perhaps Annie's. He could call himself Lockwood. Yes, that was it. He would be Strat Lockwood.

Yet if he fled, he would lose the respect of Dr. Lightner; lose his precious camera; lose Katie's letters; lose the chance to become a brilliant photographer; lose the glorious moment in which he showed Dr. Lightner the second tomb entrance he had found.

And lose, above all, the miniature envelope with the lock of Annie Lockwood's shining black hair.

Strat looked up at the peak of the Pyramid, five hundred feet above. The sky around those bronze stones was blue as a child's paint box. There had Strat knelt and asked Time to give Annie back to him.

In a few short weeks, a new century would arrive: the twentieth. Its first decade would belong to science and science alone. And here was Strat, abandoning rational thought, pretending Time was a power to move souls.

It might even be that Father was correct, and Strat *had* lost his sanity when he believed in the existence of a girl from another time.

At the dig, men were running back and forth and gesticulating. He could tell Dr. Lightner and Miss Matthews apart by their great height and he could tell his father by his great width.

Strat walked behind the Sphinx, briefly blinded by the shock of shadow. Usually when he stood by the Sphinx, the past overwhelmed him, but now he felt only the future. Future hovered around the great paws and blew sand on its back. Future gnawed its face and chewed its broken nose.

In Father's presence, he thought, my future is also broken, swallowed in the desert of his hatred. But I will not flinch from it. I will not run.

He squared his shoulders. He would not go slouching and timid into his father's presence.

The sand across which he trekked sucked at his boots and the wind tore at his face. The blue sky turned slightly yellow as the sand whirled across it.

The members of the dig saw Strat coming and they grew silent and still. Strat had the appalling thought that it was not his father of whom he must be afraid, but his companions. How could that be?

The visiting scholars, the French attaché, the Egyptians, the college boys . . . all in a row, staring at him. They looked like a firing line. Strat wanted to bolt, but kept his stride even and his face calm. He wondered what his father would say to him, after two years with no word between them.

But it was Archibald Lightner who spoke. "You lied to me, young Stratton. You claimed mere estrangement from your father. In fact, you are an escapee from an asylum, where you were incarcerated for the safety of your neighbors. You attacked and badly hurt an innocent physician who dedicated his life to helping his desperate patients. Most wretchedly, you kidnapped an innocent girl and defiled her to accomplish your escape."

That he could be accused of hurting Katie! Katie whom he loved as a sister! And that anybody could call Dr. Wilmott a dedicated innocent physician! The man was a monster who had delighted in torturing the helpless, smiling as they suffered.

Anyway, Strat had just hit him over the head with a lamp. Far from being badly hurt, Dr. Wilmott gave chase himself.

"And *now*," cried Dr. Lightner, "you have defiled my excavation!"

Strat could not believe that statement. What of his contribution to the dig? His photographs, saving for all time the accomplishments of the entire group?

"You stole that gold sandal," accused Dr. Lightner. "You squirreled it away in your own bag. You who travel so lightly, burdened only with lies, no doubt planning to run away and continue your life against society."

The insult was too deep to be borne. That he would take a possession belonging to another man? Never!

The wind rose higher, engulfing them in dust, drying their throats and hurting their eyes, making them hotter and angrier.

At last the father spoke to the son he had not seen in

two years. "I had you found," said Hiram Stratton. "I hired a detective. I plan to bring you back to America to stand trial for kidnapping and attempted murder. I considered the possibility that you were attempting to become a better person and thus deserved mercy. But I arrive to find you are a common thief."

"Father, I stole nothing. I never have. Nor did I hurt Katie in any way."

"I stand here as future patron to this excavation," thundered his father, "and this is what I must deal with first. The low base treachery of my own son."

Patron? Impossible. His father had never shown generosity. Unless, of course, he got something in exchange. And what might that be? The Stratton name on a museum wing? Strat doubted that his father had ever entered a museum.

"You stole the gold," said his father. "Nor can you deny it. You hid it deep inside your own miserable pile of clothing." Gladly, he waved the gold sandal as proof.

Strat, aghast, looked at his former friends. They met his eyes steadily and with contempt. "I found it," said the boy from Princeton. "Hidden among your clothes."

How could it have gotten there? It could only be that he had some enemy; some person in this very company who wished to destroy him.

His eyes sought understanding, and found it immediately. Miss Matthews, head and shoulders above the gloating bulk of Hiram Stratton, was staring out into the desert, cheeks red, chin high and eyes wet.

She stole the sandal, thought Strat, and made it look as if I did. She must be the detective Father hired. Father paid her to make me a thief.

Poor Dr. Lightner, in love with one who betrayed people for a living. There was no point in accusing her. Father paid so well. Impossible for truth to override that much money.

He faced his father again, and saw in his father's hand, almost invisible in the grip of that fat thumb and forefinger, the tiny envelope in which Strat kept Annie's lock of hair. It was the only possession Strat could never replace. Father, too, was a thief, having taken it from Strat's Bible, where it lay pressed when he did not keep it against his heart.

He made the error of showing that it mattered. Father, quick to see the weakness of others, opened the envelope and shook out the contents. The wind, which swirled around knees and raced, dust-laden, through shirts, now whisked away the silken tresses of Annie's hair and flung them out across the sand.

Strat's heart opened as if a wrench had been applied, turning until his valves burst and his heart broke.

"It is my belief," said the French attaché, stepping forward, "that you are also a murderer, young Stratton. Tell us how the two young men fell from the Pyramid."

"I thought it was an accident!" cried Dr. Lightner's Yale aide.

"Surely it was just carelessness," said one of the Germans, who had little use for the standards of the French.

"It was the work of ghosts," said an Egyptian.

"You heard Mr. Stratton," argued the French attaché. "In America, the boy tried to kill. In Egypt, he succeeded."

Just so had false accusations landed Strat in the asylum. His father was an expert at arranging the lies of strangers. Strat thought of Annie, who had saved him once. The wind increased, so that the sand it flung was painful to bare skin. All of Strat was raw: heart and hope. There was no Annie to save him this time, and he would never have wanted her here. She was the very reason Father had had him locked up, and Father would recognize her. He trembled to think what Hiram Stratton, Sr., would do to her. Desperately, Strat revoked his plea to Time.

"We will lock him up," said the French attaché grandly, looking forward to having an American behind bars.

"No, *we* will lock him up," said a British army officer, appalled that the French might have any power in a British protectorate.

"No," said Dr. Lightner decisively. "This has occurred in my establishment and it is my choice to put the young man under house arrest. He will not be shackled nor placed under lock and key. He will not be handed over to Egyptian authorities nor British. I wish to give you the opportunity, young Stratton, to demonstrate that you are a man of honor. Should you run, it will be proof of guilt. An innocent man has nothing to run from."

This is like a witch hunt in Old Salem, thought Strat. If I am innocent, I will be taken home to be punished. If I am guilty, I will be taken home to be punished.

But the gentlemen of Egypt, France, Italy, England, Germany and America, to whom honor was everything, awaited his response.

"I give you my word," said Strat quietly. "I am under house arrest. Under house arrest I will stay."

# CAMILLA

Camilla forced herself to look at the young man Katie had asked her to honor. Instead, Camilla had wronged him. The son was innocent of all charges, past and present. Far from avenging her own father, Camilla had sunk to the level of Strat's father.

She must find a way to save Strat. If nothing more, she owed Katie that.

But a curious thing was happening. The boy seemed to have forgotten his accusers and his witnesses. He had turned slightly, and was staring toward the Pyramid, looking at once both bewildered and excited. He took a quick shocked breath and held it, his shoulders high and motionless.

Camilla, too, looked toward the Pyramid. She caught a glimpse of shining gold, half-seen, as through gauze. There was a rasp of shoes on sand and a girl's laughter, half-heard, as through a door. It was Time, leaving its ghosts and passing on.

Camilla did not faint, but she lost strength and balance. People cried, "Are you all right?" and said to one another, "It's the heat. Put her in the shade. Put a wet cloth on her forehead."

Hiram Stratton, Sr., having lost his son's attention, grabbed Strat's arm. When Strat jerked free, all the men jumped forward to prevent a fight. Or perhaps to encourage one.

Miss Matthews was walked into her tent by Dr. Lightner, for only he was tall enough to take her arm. Dr. Lightner ducked beneath the tent flap and set her gently on the edge of her cot. Anxiously, he fanned her face with the brim of his canvas hat. Through the tent opening, she could see the broken nose of the Sphinx.

To every tourist the Sphinx was a mystery that must be plumbed. All paused before it to cry, Who are you? From whence do you spring?

Who am I? thought Camilla Matthews. I who rejected my gender, my family, my honor and my faith.

Egyptians had worshiped the Nile and the sun, their kings and their mummified cats. How strange and marvelous were all religions: the eternal need to find greater substance.

Camilla had shrugged over greater things. Immersing herself in low and ugly deeds, she had created a low and ugly situation. "Oh, Dr. Lightner," she said desperately. "I must confess that I have done a terrible thing."

"Nonsense," he said roundly. "Here. A damp cloth will cool your thoughts."

Pressing the comforting cotton against her burning eyes, Camilla made her confession. "I set young Mr.

Stratton up for this crime. I took that gold sandal. Yes, it was I. I placed it in the young man's trunk so you would blame him. He is innocent."

Relief washed over Camilla. At last, she had done a good thing. She might be flung out of camp or thrown onto the next ship. She even might be the one sent to prison. But at least Strat would not suffer at her hands. She risked a humiliated glance at Dr. Lightner.

But he was regarding her with great esteem. A soft smile crossed his face. "Nothing," said Dr. Lightner, "is so beautiful as a woman who sacrifices for a man. Miss Matthews, how kind and generous is your feminine heart. You wish to save the boy from punishment. How I respect you. But no one will believe that trumped-up story. Your truthfulness and honor are visible to all who have met you."

It had not occurred to Camilla that she would not be believed. "Truly, sir, it was my doing. I committed the act."

"Now, now. You have enough troubles merely enduring the great heat. Ladies should not be here at this time of year. As for the theft of the sandal, it is too much for your feminine sensibilities to accept that some men are evil and do evil things. I think it best for your sake to remove you to Lady Clementine's abode. She delighted in your company, as of course do I, but her villa is better for you than this hot and dusty encampment."

"But you must explain to everyone, Dr. Lightner, what really happened. Especially it must be made clear to the French, who have jumped to dreadful conclusions."

"Dear girl, we know what really happened. Young Stratton is his father all over again. I fear he does not deserve your assistance. One day he too will clench a cigar in his teeth, looking and smelling like the smokestack of his factory. He too will burn down that factory in order to get his way."

Camilla gave a little cry and hid once more behind his handkerchief.

"You know of that fire?" His arm had gone around her shoulder and she felt the comforting heat of his body. "That factory burned when I was in America raising money for this expedition," he told her. "Innocent people died in that fire. I'm told there was no investigation. Mr. Stratton simply paid off everyone involved."

Not everyone, thought Camilla. I wonder if Mama would have accepted his money, if he had offered it, to keep us in school. I accepted money from him. Passing it through Mr. Duffie's hands does not cleanse it. I am a sinner with my hands dipped in Stratton money.

Oh, there were too many moral problems here, and she without her church. "I do not think young Strat is like his father," she said. Tears filled her eyes, she who was supposed to be like a man and never weep. She could not help quoting Katie. "I think he is a good and decent and generous boy."

She was talking as if she really were a decade older than Strat, but in fact she was two years younger.

Remembering that she was only seventeen made her want to behave seventeen, and weep on Dr. Lightner's shoulder, and be taken care of. But that was not her lot in life, and she must not weaken.

Dr. Lightner burst out, "How touched I am by your tender heart! No matter what your height and frame say of boldness and strength, in fact you are gentle and full of love. Willing to sacrifice so that a young man might go free! Oh, Miss Matthews."

Camilla had completed the task of making him fall in love with her, weeks ahead of schedule. He was too good for her and she must walk away from him, but perhaps she could use the trap she had set for Dr. Lightner to undo the trap she had set for Strat.

"Honored sir," said Camilla shakily, "might we discuss a way to extricate the boy from his father's grasp? Such a wicked man does not tell the truth. I believe Hiram Stratton lies even about his son. I believe there were no such events as the kidnapping and the attack. Please. Let us conjure a way to set Strat free."

Dr. Lightner fiddled with some shards of pottery on which undeciphered hieroglyphs awaited his expertise. His thumb stroked letters incised thousands of years ago by a scribe. "If you have fallen in love with the young man, Miss Matthews," he said bravely, "I will do all within my power to assist you in saving him."

Camilla dropped the handkerchief and all pretense. How gallant he was! And how she agreed that nothing was more beautiful than one person sacrificing for another. "I have fallen in love with you, sir. But I am in a position to know that the father is truly evil and to extricate the son I do require your utmost assistance."

Dr. Lightner wrapped her hand tightly in his and kissed the top of it. "Do you mean that?" he whispered. "That you—that you—" The words were too intimate to be repeated.

Camilla nodded.

"Here is a way out then," he said. He patted her hair and cheeks, afraid to overstep his rights, but too emotional to keep a correct distance. "The British love war so very deeply. The wars in India have run out, and war in the Sudan may end within days, but luckily, war looms in South Africa. Those Dutchmen down there, Boers they call themselves, are trying to throw the British out. Everybody is happy. There's nothing like a good fight. I shall suggest young Stratton to my British friends as a cameraman. Off he goes to fight the Dutch. Thousands of miles once more between him and his father. This time we shall see that he uses a false name."

It was perfect! Strat would be saved. On her way back to America, Camilla would disembark in Spain to give Katie money and news. She would tell the truth about her own foul deeds and then she would find the priest of the convent at the hospital, and tell him the truth also. She would get her religion back if she got nothing else, and once home, she would no longer spy for Mr. Duffie. Somehow she would keep her brothers in school, but not that way.

Maybe I really could sell my first article as Strat sold his first picture, she thought, and from there go on to a splendid career. I shall be a spinster, but with fewer regrets, for I shall shine on my own.

Dr. Lightner stood. "I shall go then, and see how this may be managed."

Camilla looked into his face and immediately had more, not fewer, regrets. She did not want to be a spinster. She wanted Archibald Lightner. "And the French?" she said, jumping up. "What about their silly accusation?"

"Please, my dear. Sit back down and rest. The heat tired you."

"I'm over it," said Camilla crossly. "How will you handle the French?" She opened the tent flap for him instead of the other way around.

He laughed. "I don't know yet. First, let's make sure the young man himself will go along with our plan."

# STRAT

The gold sandal had been set upon the dusty table where Dr. Lightner wrote up his notes in the evening. It seemed to Strat that the slipper actually sang: an ancient high quaver, a golden voice from the past. He touched the delicately incised gold rope under which a girl's toes had once slid.

Strat's heart actually stopped. It hit his ribs once, with a huge thrust of energy, and then it ceased to beat.

*Annie had worn that sandal.*

Around him, the figures and their speech glazed, as raw umber over oils on a painting. The angry men grew solid and still, fixing themselves as people on paper. There was light and shadow and heat. There was not sound.

A camel train appeared on the horizon, like liquid slowly poured over the sand, long black shadows spilled behind.

And Strat spilled out of the picture, falling and tumbling, like the French boys from the top of the Pyramid. His bones smashed against its rocky sides, and Strat could not understand this, because he was not on the

179

Pyramid, but on the sand. His skin was laid open by the scrape and assault of the stones. His mind broke apart, thoughts scattered like seed from a clumsy hand.

He spun into the vortex of the past. There were faces with him: hideous, unknown others being wrenched through Time.

And then he hit bottom, and it was stone.

# CAMILLA

The members of Dr. Lightner's dig were turning in circles in the sand, like dogs deciding whether to lie down. The German scholars and the French attaché were puzzled and embarrassed. They could not produce Strat for Dr. Lightner and Miss Matthews.

"Where did you put your son?" Camilla demanded of Mr. Stratton. "Surely you have not already incarcerated him? It was agreed that he would stay upon his honor."

Mr. Stratton was bewildered and angry. "He was here a moment ago."

"He ran," opined the French attaché.

"He couldn't have," objected the Yale assistant. "He must be here. We'll help you look, Miss Matthews."

But nobody could find Strat. There was not a trace of him.

"He has fled," said Dr. Lightner sadly.

"Proof of guilt!" said Hiram Stratton gladly.

"Strat said he would put himself under house arrest,"

said Camilla through stiff lips. "He will be back by dark. He gave his word, and I accept that."

Oh, Strat, she thought, if you are not back . . .

No man here will forgive you for breaking your word. Even Dr. Lightner may refuse to help you after all.

# STRAT

Above Strat spread a sky vast and dark, pierced by a thousand stars and a sliver of moon. Torches burned in tall posts, illuminating pyramid, pillar and stone.

He stood exactly where he had been standing in another time, fifty feet from the causeway. He had arrived at the beginning, when Khufu's Pyramid was perfect. It was a ghost, or he was.

Strat's breath came in shallow spurts, as if he were afraid of antique air. Slowly his lungs returned, his legs and strength, and he could feel again the sweet beating of his heart.

He was surrounded by temples and mastabas and monuments he could not identify because they did not exist in 1899. He could not see the Sphinx. The causeway, mostly destroyed or buried in his time, was lined with statues, covered by awnings and scented by flowers in massive pots.

He became aware of a steady, rhythmic tapping. He turned and looked toward the Nile. The sound of feet marching, he decided; guards, perhaps, walking back and forth during their night watch. Partially visible through the tall pillars of an open temple, motionless in the water of a lagoon that had vanished long before Strat's time, lay a large and well-lit boat. Although he judged the hour to be very late, there was a good deal of activity on its deck.

It seemed best not to attract attention. Strat stayed well away from the torchlight.

First he would examine the Pyramid. He had climbed it, photographed it, fallen in love with it—but only its core. Think of seeing it as Khufu's architects had planned! Strat was astonished to see a wall around the Pyramid, with the obvious intent of preventing visitors from scaling the monument. The year 1899 had its advantages after all; you need not just stand at the bottom and stare up.

Suddenly he saw the Sphinx. It existed, not half-broken, but half-carved.

O mystery of mysteries, thought Strat reverently. You are a creation of man, and that man must be Khufu!

He was startled by a sudden clatter and some sharply issued orders.

In ancient Egyptian! He was thrilled. He strained to hear, for nobody in 1899 knew how to pronounce the words so painstakingly translated from hieroglyphs.

A phalanx of soldiers was forming near the lagoon. They marched through the temple, pivoted sharply and turned onto the causeway. Their boots and the shafts of their spears slammed against the pavement. Strat drew deeper in the shadows. There were not many soldiers, and yet the sound they made was the sound of many: the relentless echo of men who would show no mercy and give no quarter . . . men not unlike his own father.

The procession was both beautiful and threatening. In the midst of the soldiers was carried a huge litter. Strat could not see the occupant, but he recognized the tall crown from tomb paintings: the headgear of the Lord of the Two Lands.

*Pharaoh.*

The man was so motionless in his litter that Strat decided this was a representation of the Lord of the Two Lands, and not the king himself.

All too aware of his khaki-colored trousers and shirt, Strat dropped down into the sand, that he might cast no shadow. The sand was cold, having no capacity to hold heat. The desert that had failed to roast a man by day tried to freeze him by night. Strat shivered. Farther out in the sand, a high vicious yapping began.

A pack of wild dogs? No, he thought, this is Egypt. *Jackals.*

The jackals were much too close and far too interested. Also not unlike his father.

Next in the procession came men who seemed neither soldier nor priest, another litter and more soldiers.

Fearful of discovery, Strat inched backward over the sand, although moving into range of the jackals did not seem wise either. But the parade stopped well away from him. They did not pause in front of one of the temples or mastabas or baby pyramids. They gathered, it seemed to Strat, around a shadowy circle in the causeway itself.

He squinted to see better, and writhed in the sand for a better angle. It looked like a manhole, like a—

Strat was embarrassed. This was ancient Egypt. There was no room for confusion under these circumstances. It must be a tomb entrance.

Pharaoh's litter was set down. Soldiers assisted Pharaoh out of it. They removed his crown and he himself swung off his cape. So he was real. His chest was as hung with medals and ribbons and sashes as any British officer bound for war. He was spectacular.

There were prayers, with hands held up to the sky; there was anointing with oil; there was sharing of the cup.

From the second litter, two girls in white gowns were brought forward. One knelt, kissed the ground, and sang from a kneeling position. The cool high notes of her psalm rang between the vast stones, echoing in the night air. Was she a priestess? A daughter or wife of Khufu?

Strat knew the name of Khufu's mother, Hetepheres; he was sure he could hear those syllables in the girl's song. Now he recognized the notes. It was the song of the gold sandal, when he had held it in his hands.

As the ceremony went on, ropes were rigged. Two rock slabs were hauled across the sand, each perhaps four feet across and six or eight inches thick. Heavy, but nothing compared to the two-ton stones that made up the Pyramid. Many baskets, also containing something very heavy, were carried up.

The second girl sang nothing and did nothing, but stood motionless. She wore so much gold that she herself was scarcely visible.

Now Khufu himself spoke, and even the jackals were silent as Pharaoh expanded his voice, and his orders filled the City of the Dead.

The singer was lifted into a sort of basket on ropes and lowered gently into the tomb. The girl wrapped in gold was put into the next basket and also lowered. Torches dipped forward, in fascination or reverence. There was a great spill of light and the second girl was no longer shadow under jewels. Strat could see her features and her eyes.

It was Annie.

He had hardly begun rejoicing at the marvelous ways of Time—the miraculous conjunction of souls—the perfect meeting soon to occur in the perfect place— when the next lowering into the shaft occurred.

It was not a priest or a soldier who went down. It was the first rock-hewn slab.

Promptly, the second slab was lowered over the first, and the men began a great and dreadful warbling. They hooted like robed birds gone mad, bowing and nodding to the earth. Then, one by one, man by man, they emptied the baskets down the shaft. Sand and rock and pebble.

Filling it.

# ANNIE

Annie and Renifer were in a small room with a large bed. The pile of soft pillows awaited. So did death.

It was a parody of a slumber party. But they had not dressed Annie for a party. They had dressed her for eternity.

She did not speak to Renifer and Renifer did not speak to her, because they shared no language and because there was nothing to say.

Annie took off the magnificent necklace, the crown, the thick bracelets, the anklets and amulets. She laid them in a row at the foot of the bed. Gold was beautiful, but you could not, in fact, take it with you. When she slithered out of the netted gown, its bright beads tumbled onto the floor, tangled beyond hope. She slid out of the gold sandals but when her bare feet touched the stone floor, she couldn't stand it. There might be spiders or beetles or rats down here. So she kept the sandals on and fingered the pleats in her stiff white undergown.

Time, you vicious spirit. How could you do this to me? Renifer's torch will burn out. We will sit in the dark while we suffocate.

Annie had contemplated death, of course. All thinking people contemplate death. Her own age was particularly fascinated with it. Whenever they had a poetry assignment, half the kids wrote about death. But none of them ever expected to sit inside their own tomb with lots of time to consider the future of their own dead body.

I am going to become a mummy, she thought.

Annie had read that the Egyptians had not really needed to mummify their dead; the desert would do it for them. Egypt was so dry that bodies behaved like autumn leaves, turning color and turning crispy.

The torch had burned down too low for Renifer to hold it anymore. She set the bit of flaming wood against the stone sarcophagus, where it burned brightly, casting shadows along the incised hieroglyphs. The ceiling was quite high. Annie watched the smoke rise. Perhaps she should breathe deeply and get it over with.

It was uncommon for an American to feel helpless. Annie's generation and country did not believe in that kind of thing. If you had character and intelligence, you did not permit yourself to be helpless. You solved everything.

Annie would not solve this.

She would not solve thirst, hunger, fear or rage. She would not teach Renifer to speak English, so they could mourn together. She would not dismantle the tomb from the inside, nor tug away granite slabs as large as picnic tables and then empty the shaft so she could climb up.

Instead, she would listen to her heartbeat and wonder what it would be like when that stopped. And then it would stop.

The torch flickered. Annie did not think she could bear being in total dark. "Renifer," she whispered.

Renifer took Annie into her arms and sang gently, as in a lullabye.

Rock me to sleep, thought Annie. Let me not remember in my sleep that I have been buried alive. Let me not wake, but just drift away and not have to feel what is happening to me.

And as she fell asleep, she understood what Time had done.

In 1899, Strat was going to dig up bones that had been interred for thousands of years.

And they would be Annie's.

# VI

*Time to Die*

# RENIFER

Renifer hoped she would be the first to die. It was bad enough to lie next to an empty sarcophagus in the dark. She didn't want to lie next to the corpse of the girl of ivory. Renifer's mouth was dry. Thirst was not yet torture, but that would come. She and the girl of ivory would not die easily.

She could neither pray nor summon happy memories. The image of her mother shopping, her little brothers playing ball, her sister stealing her eye makeup, her girlfriends casting eyes at Pankh—none of these could she remember.

She pictured instead the hand of her father dropping a rock as his contribution to the sealing of his living daughter's tomb. The smile of Pankh as he took his turn. How Pharaoh would honor them. How their careers would soar.

I do not mind dying for thee, O queen, thought Renifer. But to die while Father and Pankh laugh at Pharaoh! To die neither embalmed nor prayed over, while Father and Pankh are given tombs in the best part of the City of the Dead. I mind that.

Pankh had not spoken to Renifer as she was led to her fate. He had touched his forehead to the ground at Pharaoh's feet, but he had not touched the cheek or hand of his beloved. Nor had he touched the girl of ivory. His eyes had done that for him: caressing the gold she wore. In Pankh's eyes had been heat and excitement such as Renifer herself had never generated.

It was lust for gold.

Pankh will rob this tomb, thought Renifer.

He would wait until the girls were dead. He would wait a month or year. Until Pharaoh was busy with other affairs. Until new guards had been given new bribes. Until the gold he already possessed was not enough and he must have more.

He would empty the shaft. It would take several nights. He would remove rubble, cart it away, temporarily plaster over the cavity, open it up again the next night. Lifting the two slabs at the bottom would be easy, since the ropes still lay tied around them. He would step over the bodies, pleased that the girl of ivory had stripped off her gold and stacked it so neatly.

His wife would wear it. For Pankh would marry soon. His station required it. Possibly he would marry Renifer's little sister, thus keeping the secrets in the family.

In the darkness, Renifer inched away from the sleeping pale girl and went to her knees and prayed.

*Sekhmet! Destroy Pankh who destroys queens. Destroy him who loves gold more than love. I beg thee, in honor of my willing sacrifice, with thy power, make him suffer.*

Renifer sat back on her heels, hugging her knees to

her chest. Never had she been so sure that a prayer had been heard.

She sat in terrible darkness, where not even gold had value, and dreamed of what Sekhmet would do to Pankh. And then began the terror. Not for Pankh, who deserved it! For Renifer herself.

*Queen Hetepheres began to open her sarcophagus from the inside.*

There was a creaking of bones as joints moved, and the sound of old dead laughter.

Renifer imagined the fingernails of a dead queen raking her face.

But Father had destroyed the mummy! There was no queen within that coffin.

The girl of ivory awoke and they gripped each other in the dreadful dark.

No longer did the sound seem to come from the sarcophagus. It was on all sides: above and below, left and right.

Was it the sound of a *ka* rejoining its mummy? But there was no mummy to find!

What rage would the *ka* exhibit when it learned the evil truth? It seemed to be trapped in the walls, fighting in the shaft, scrabbling on the surface. What would it do to Renifer and the girl of ivory when it got into the room with them?

Renifer prayed aloud, desperate to reach the ears of the coming *ka*. "No," she prayed. "O queen, I gave myself for you. I die for you. Do not attack me in the dark. O grandmother of Meresankh, whom I served, pity me!"

There were grunts and scrabbles. Scrapes and moans. A trickle, as of many pebbles; and a cry, as of pain.

I would rather have been impaled in the desert in the sun, thought Renifer. At least I could see and understand my death.

Beloved gods! Do not allow the fingers of the dead to feel the skin of my face.

# PANKH

Pankh was permitted the honor of escorting Pharaoh back to the royal barge. The royal hand lay upon Pankh's forehead; the royal blessing bestowed upon Pen-Meru. But already Pharaoh's mind was elsewhere. His mother was safe and now He must get a good night's sleep.

Pankh did not consider Pharaoh a fool. The Lord of the Two Lands was as strong a king as Egypt had known. But He believed too much in His own people. He believed in loyalty.

It was Pankh's experience that men were more loyal to gold than to kings. A hundred men had gasped at the sight of that gold. Chains of gold, circles of gold, hanks of gold, crowns of gold—draped upon the girl of ivory, who neither bent nor sagged, but stood white and flawless, a statue of marble, carrying it into eternity.

Or . . . as long as it took for tomb robbers to relieve her of the burden.

Pharaoh went to His chamber. The procession

dispersed. Torches were doused. Priests went to their beds. Soldiers changed watch. Pen-Meru was rowed to Memphis, his arms full of treasure to replace his daughter.

Pankh, however, drifted toward the docks and piers. He knew the waterfront well. The dark was his friend. Half a mile upstream, he eased out into the desert. Silently and carefully, he circled the City of the Dead, keeping to the shadows, more uneasy about jackals than tomb police. He would approach the girls' tomb from the vacant western desert instead of the busy Nile.

Pankh would not be the only one who wanted that gold, but he was definitely the only one bold enough to take it the very same night Pharaoh dedicated it. In Pharaoh's own procession had been at least one tomb guard and one priest known to assist robbers. But did these men know there was a second shaft? That it had not been filled? Did they know the exact location? Or would it take them years of poking to locate the spot?

Pankh had purchased the architect's plans for the tomb of Princess Nitiqret of Blessed Memory. But that did not mean the plans had been sold only once.

He must retrieve the gold before dawn. At the sun's first rays, the next police shift would arrive. Priests would be performing morning ablutions, tourists gawking, families picnicking. Acolytes would be anxiously reporting for their first day and vendors setting up their tables to sell cheap straw hats. The girl of ivory had worn so much gold! But if she could wear that much, he could carry or hide that much.

Pankh slipped among the minor pyramids to find the second shaft.

He regretted that the girls would not yet be dead.

In a way, he reasoned, it would be an act of generosity to speed them on their way. Less suffering. Yes, he was being kind.

# ANNIE

Annie and Renifer were holding each other so tightly she could not tell whose heart was pounding so loudly: her own, Renifer's, or the intruder's.

It was the dark that was so very terrible. Although she had looked around carefully when there was still torchlight, and knew how small was the room in which they were trapped, higher than it was wide, now that it was utterly dark, she did not know. She could not bring herself to reach forth in the pitch black and touch a wall or a floor and the ceiling was far too high to be touched.

And then, through her fear, she became aware of something most odd. She felt a strong draft. There should not be fresh air in a sealed tomb, let alone a breeze.

Somehow, somewhere, an airway had been opened. Only the hand of man could move rocks and let in a draft. So . . . the scrapes—could those be rocks as they were dragged away? The grunts—from a living man's chest? The rasping—soles of shoes sliding down stone?

Could this be *rescue*?

But who would rescue them?

She understood now that Pharaoh had ordered their deaths. His soldiers would not march back to retrieve the sacrifice. The priests had been proud to participate. In the faces of all assembled, Annie had seen reverence.

That left Pankh and Pen-Meru. Had Annie misjudged them? Were they good people after all? Helpless to act when surrounded by Pharaoh's finest soldiers? Had they returned, at hideous risk to themselves, to save Renifer?

If it is them, thought Annie, they'll save Renifer, but they won't save me. I'm the sacrifice. They'll leave me here.

The draft lifted her hair. Whoever was coming had opened a considerable airway.

And I'm climbing up it, she told herself. Pankh buried me alive; I have the right to smash him in the head.

She still wore the gold sandals. She slid one off and gripped it firmly in her hand. It was a good solid weapon. She'd knock him out in the dark and shinny out of her tomb.

There was a long scraping drag as stone was pulled over stone.

Trembling, the girls waited. Annie had lost any sense of direction in the little room and did not know where to look to find the shaft down which they had been lowered. But light, when she saw it at last, did not appear in the wall where the shaft had been. It was in the ceiling. A stone was being dragged away and slowly a slit was appearing. Fingers gripped the edge of the stone and shifted it more. Grunts and gasps followed. The fingers vanished, and returned gripping a torch.

Behind the murky smoke that swirled up to fresh air and life was a dark and half-seen face.

If Pankh can get down, I can get up, she said to herself. She had not a moment to waste. Lifting the magnificent sedan chair on which Queen Hetepheres had once rested, she hauled it onto the high bed and propped it against the headboard.

Above her, the torch was set on the edge of the hole. Pankh could not both hold the torch and lower himself. He sat on the edge of the hole above her and came down feet first. Annie tightened her grip on the sandal and climbed up onto the sedan chair. She was high enough to break Pankh's kneecaps, but not high enough to smash in his skull. Perhaps she should just break his fingers off.

Annie had never had impressive upper arm strength. She prayed adrenaline would give her enough kick so she could haul herself up into the hole.

The soiled shoelaces of Pankh's scratchy old leather boots had come undone.

I could grab him by the feet and yank him down, she thought. If I'm lucky, he'll break his spine on the floor.

She drew her arm back, preparing to whack him with all her might.

An inch of bright red sock showed at the top of the boots. The legs were encased in khaki trousers with frayed hems. She had not seen Pankh in anything but bare legs and a little white kilt.

The body lowered.

Annie held her sandal at the ready.

A waist appeared, and its belt. A shirt appeared, and its buttons. Elbows unfolded. Hanging from his fingers was Strat.

"Don't hit me," he said.

She could not speak. She could neither laugh nor cry. She could not even touch him, because with one hand she held her weapon and with the other was steadying herself against the wall.

"You're beautiful," he said to her.

She nodded. "Fit for a king," she told him.

"I was there. I saw. It was Khufu, wasn't it?"

"Who cares about him? Oh, Strat! How did you get here? Where did you come from! I was scared of death and pain and darkness and then there was all that noise and I thought you were a mummy coming out of the sarcophagus."

"In 1899 when we open that sarcophagus," said Strat, "there is no mummy. It's something of a mystery. I can't hang here much longer, Annie. It's either let go or haul back up."

"If you let go, you're going to spike yourself on the bedstead. I'll hop down from the sedan chair and move the furniture."

It didn't work that easily. She broke the arm of the chair by stepping wrong and fell backward onto the mattress. Strat kicked the sedan chair off the bed and fell onto the mattress with her.

She felt his face, every inch of it, to be sure this was

her Strat, the one she remembered so vividly, the one she had wanted so very very much. He caught her long hair in his knotted fist and kissed her. "Oh, Annie. Of all the terrible things that happened, the worst was losing your lock of hair. All this time, I have cherished it. And this afternoon, my father threw it into the wind and it vanished in the desert."

They clung to each other.

"You got away, then?" Annie said to him. "You escaped Dr. Wilmott and all the dangers that pursued you? I never knew. I could only guess and hope."

"Oh, Annie, it was just so for me. Did you suffer after we parted? Did I behave wrongly? I have agonized over it," he said. "It was a terrible decision, and so little time in which to make it. But I had to save Katie. You were strong and could survive. Katie was fragile and could not." He kissed her cheeks and lips, her throat and hair.

Even now he cannot overstep the bounds of propriety, thought Annie.

How she loved him!

"I begged Time to let me see you again, Annie," he said, feasting his eyes on her. The torch, still lying on the edge of the hole in the upper room, gave a faint shadowy glow to the room. "I climbed to the top of Khufu's Pyramid to ask it, because the natives say that the ghosts of Time are present in the night." He tightened his embrace.

In his time, a lady was not merely covered with undergarments of lace, silk and satin, but also strapped into corsets, so that the actual form and feel of the lady was unavailable to anybody, including the lady. Surely what his hands told him now of Annie Lockwood was beyond the bounds of propriety. He comforted himself that this was ancient Egypt, however, and for that, she was properly dressed.

"Not only did Time bring us together," said Strat, "but amid such excitement."

"If you call being buried alive excitement," said Annie. "The two of us are supposed to suffocate to death down here. I think there's a famous opera where that actually happens."

"*Aida,*" said Strat. "In days gone by I often attended such musical torture."

They held each other, their tears dampening their close cheeks.

"How did you know how to get down to us?" asked Annie. "I can't stand feeling so confused."

"I found a second shaft in real life," he told her. "Well, 1899 life. Just this morning. Except forty-five hundred years from now, if I remember Khufu's dates correctly. I paced it off exactly, and of course the same markers are here, because this came first. So Time flung me down on the sand, and I regained consciousness, and had the astounding privilege of seeing Pharaoh in a royal procession, and the shocking reality of seeing two human sacrifices, and just as the second sacrifice was lowered in her basket, I recognized her."

Annie buried her face in his throat.

He said, "I'm not sure if you were sent to save me or if I was sent to save you. Had I stayed in my time, I would have been in terrible difficulties."

"Had you stayed in your time," said Annie, "I would have been dead. Was it you the other day in the museum? Did you buy me lunch?"

He was puzzled. "Lunch?" he said confusedly. "What museum?"

"I forgot. It hasn't happened yet. But I'm sure it's you."

She had the oddest sense of wanting to get back and check on him in the museum. First, we'd better get out of our tomb, she thought, sitting up abruptly.

"Tell me how it worked for you," he said, sitting up with her. He slid his hand under the mass of her silky hair and rubbed her spine.

"Your photographs," said Annie. "You had told me you were going to Egypt to be an archaeologist, do you remember? I never found out a single thing about what happened to you. You vanished. But I happened to pick up the Sunday *New York Times,* which my parents don't often buy and I almost never touch. And I felt you through the print. You were in a museum article. So I went to the museum to find you. I have only four days, which is the first problem. You see, my parents just got married, Strat. It was a lovely ceremony, and they're having a very short honeymoon so I thought we could have a very short reunion or ask Time to stretch it or bring you back with me or stay here with you."

Strat decided not to ask why her parents had just gotten married. It seemed late, what with their daughter in her teens. But who was he, whose father was on wife number four, to quibble about the marriages of parents? "The ceremony I just watched was also lovely," he teased. "You made a beautiful sacrifice."

"Thank you," said Annie. "I threw Pharaoh's gold on the floor over there. I think, but I'm not sure, that Renifer's actual father and her actual boyfriend handed her over to Pharaoh to be sacrificed. Those two men enjoyed every minute of shoving Renifer underground."

"I cannot accept such a statement," said Strat. "Her own father? Her own beloved? I expect they were so fearful of Pharaoh that they could not move to save their darling girl."

"Since when have you thought highly of fathers?" Annie demanded. "Your own father did the same thing to you. Or have you already forgotten being thrown down the shaft, so to speak, into the asylum?"

Strat did not like to think that the world—now, then or ever—had fathers who behaved that way. He liked to think of his own father as an unpleasant exception. He liked to think that when he became a father, he would be an excellent one. Under the circumstances, both 1899 and now, however, he did not actually expect to reach adulthood and have the privilege of being a father.

"Tell me everything," said Annie. "Tell me about your life, and Devonny, and Harriett and Katie and what happened and where everybody is and all that."

"First let's get out of here," said Strat. He got up off Queen Hetepheres' bed and paced the tiny room. He smiled at Renifer, who was backed against the wall, holding her hand up to keep him away. "Don't be afraid," he said to her. "I came to save you both."

Renifer just held both hands up like traffic signals.

"I don't know how much time we have, Annie," said Strat, suddenly worried. "Dawn will come soon. We have to get up out of here, but once we are out on the sand, we'll be very visible. The soldiers won't take kindly to finding Pharaoh's sacrifices running around laughing."

"How hard will it be to get out?" asked Annie, staring up at the hole.

"Easy. I had to remove some stones, which took me a while, but once the shaft was revealed, there's a ladder. We just go up and we're fifty feet or so from Hetepheres' chapel. I'll go first, and then reach down and help each of you up."

Standing tiptoe on the bed frame, Strat was able to get his fingers around the stone rim of the ceiling hole. With the wonderful upper arm strength of boys, he hauled himself upward.

"I couldn't do that in a thousand years," said Annie.

"You don't need to," said Strat. "Hand Renifer up first."

But Renifer would not go.

# RENIFER

Renifer's heart was still beating, which she thought amazing, considering what she had been through.

The thing was male, she could tell from the voice and shape of it.

It was foreign, she could tell from the smell and clothing of it.

It was not a *ka,* because a ghost could pass through stone but this creature had needed an opening, as humans did.

Renifer had pretended that it would be Pankh, coming to prove his love. For a space of time so brief the words had hardly formed in her mind, she even asked Sekhmet to dismiss her prayer for revenge. But she had been right the first time. Pankh's love was gold, and he would come for that.

The rescuer, on the other hand, had not glanced at the treasure on the floor. It meant nothing to him. He cared about the girl. And the girl, whom Renifer had thought chained by the gold, had forgotten it also, swept away by the presence of the boy. Even now, begging, they were not thinking of gold, but of her.

They wanted to save her.

I cannot go, she said, without words, because neither of them could understand Egyptian, and because she did not think they could understand in any language. The Living God had decreed that she stay here and die. Yes, this was terror. She had felt great terror when she had stood above, and grasped what Pharaoh wanted of her. She felt greater terror in the hours of knowledge below the earth.

But now, Renifer could make the choice herself. Live or die?

Her family had betrayed Pharaoh in all ways. She, Renifer, could atone. She could die for Hetepheres.

She climbed on top of the sarcophagus, and lay down on her back, carefully adjusting her gown and folding her arms over her chest as neatly as if she had been laid out by the priests. She stared silently upward at the un-painted ceiling.

The girl of ivory begged and plucked at her and the boy called from his hole in the ceiling. Arguments in a foreign language were presented. Tears were shed. For a while, it even seemed that the boy might come back down and they would try to force Renifer into the fresh air.

How many human sacrifices had to fight for the privilege of staying dead?

"Go," said Renifer irritably. "Go!" She flicked her fingers at the girl as one might snap at a bug and hoped the girl would understand. Of course she did not, being a foreigner, and instead stamped her foot like Renifer's little sister having a tantrum.

Renifer returned her gaze to the ceiling. She was faintly amused by what was happening. Hetepheres' reburial had been arranged so speedily that none of the priests and courtiers on the barge and none of the soldiers at the shaft had paused to remember that an unused tomb probably had more than one open shaft. In a week or a year, some dedicated priest of Pharaoh would remember.

But would he do anything?

Renifer doubted it. Innocent men had already died because of Hetepheres' tomb. Why be numbered among them?

A dedicated priest might even decide to check that second shaft and fill it in himself, to be sure the queen's tomb could not be robbed yet again. But Renifer had recognized Pharaoh's priest last night. It was the man who had held his ostrich fan in front of his face, fleeing the unfortunate event of Pen-Meru caught in the act of robbing Hetepheres' tomb. No doubt that priest was very dedicated. To gold.

Which meant there had been at least three tomb robbers present at the reburial of Hetepheres: the priest, her father, her beloved. Poor Pharaoh, she thought. You do not know with whom You consort.

"Renifer!" said the girl of ivory fiercely, trying to drag her right off the sarcophagus.

Renifer made a universal sign: finger slicing her throat. Quit!

Muttering, the girl expended considerable effort replacing the queen's sedan chair on top of the mattress.

At first Renifer thought the girl was going to do a little tomb robbing after all, but then she understood the girl wanted to be sure that Renifer could change her mind. If Renifer stood on top of that sedan chair, she might be close enough to the ceiling to pull herself through.

Coming back to the sarcophagus, the girl kissed her own fingertips and placed those fingertips on Renifer's forehead, drawing on her skin a sign Renifer did not recognize. A blessing, perhaps, or a salute. Renifer would never know. She did not let herself meet the girl's eyes. In a moment of weakness, she might surrender, cry out and go with them.

Pankh was weak. She, Renifer, would be strong.

She held her breath and all her muscle and bone against weakness and while she lay rigid and unyielding, the boy lifted his girl into the upper chamber. A treasure room empty, Renifer supposed, of anything except air.

Although, in its way, air was a treasure.

The boy did not slide the stone over the ceiling opening. She would lie here knowing she could leave, and that was difficult knowledge to possess. The flow of fresh air meant that she could not die easily in gathering sleep, and would die in the dreadful pain of thirst. But they were foreigners, and did not understand these things, and she had no means to explain.

She could tell by the sounds of their feet that a ladder remained in place inside the shaft; that he went first and she second up the shaft and from thence to freedom and life.

And then they were gone.

Renifer's tears puddled on the cold stone at her back. Then she prayed, composing a song for her own soul. How glorious and magnified was her voice in the stone chamber. She imagined her soprano rising like smoke, ascending to heaven, and knew that Pharaoh would be pleased.

She decided to die wearing Pharaoh's gold, so that when she passed into the next world, she could present that gold to Hetepheres and be acquitted of the evil deeds of her family.

She dressed slowly, finishing just as the torch the boy had left by the ceiling hole went out.

The weight of the gold was great. She feared falling over, getting disoriented in the dark or hurting herself. She wanted to die in dignity. So, keeping a grip on the edge of the sarcophagus to steady herself, Renifer knelt to pray once more.

She asked for one thing only.

That Hetepheres' tomb should not be robbed twice.

# PANKH

Pankh pressed his back against a small obelisk, faced directly west and counted paces. He need only kick aside a few rocks, breaking the plaster that held them together, and shift a few large flat stones. According to the plans, these were not slabs requiring a team of men or ropes.

The torches on the causeway had been doused by the priests themselves to provide secrecy for the reburial of Hetepheres. Pankh felt his way through the gloom and shadows toward the entrance to the second shaft. He had almost finished the pace count when he saw on the ground a darker dark. A hole.

Somebody else had gotten to the second shaft before him. His hand flew to the hilt of his dagger. *That gold is mine,* he thought. *I will kill them!*

He was already making plans: better, perhaps, to shove the stones back over the hole, entrapping the robbers, and wait a few weeks, when both tomb robbers *and* girls would have died! Or perhaps he should just join the ongoing robbery. At least he would get some of the gold.

Although Pankh did not share well, and still meant to have it all.

But a hand stopped him.

Pankh whirled, ready to slash, and found himself facing two puzzled tomb police. If they were part of the robbery, they would have knifed him from behind. So they were simply doing their jobs, wondering who was wandering around in the dark, and why.

Luckily, he was wearing his best clothing and his finest jewelry. His uniform would give him some control. "Good evening," he said, smiling, and guiding them away from the half-visible hole. "What good luck that you have appeared," he told them. "Perhaps you would spend a moment or two to help me."

He managed to draw them around the corner of an old mastaba, with flat roof and sloping sides. To face him, the police would have their backs to the shaft opening. "I dropped an amulet of Sekhmet during Pharaoh's night ceremony, the one finished only an hour or two ago, in which I was honored to participate. I hoped to see my amulet still lying here."

Pankh sneered at amulets and religious symbols. When men or women hung such things about their necks, or built little shrines in their gardens, or more comical still, erected temples, Pankh laughed. Tomb robbers were atheists and knew what the common run of people did not. Nothing mattered except possessions.

"Why don't we wait for the sun to rise," said one policeman, "so we can see better?"

In the east, the sand had brightened. In a moment,

dawn would explode over the desert. Surely Pankh was not too late to get the gold! "Let's go over to the causeway," he suggested, herding them. "I'm sure my precious amulet is lying on the stones."

"Then why were you coming from the desert?" asked one policeman pleasantly.

"The Lord of the Two Lands required a sacrifice to the jackals and to Anubis, jackal god of the dead, because of the urgency of Pharaoh's prayers and the need for celestial guidance."

The guards were unconvinced. He did manage to jostle them onto the causeway, however.

"Here it is!" exclaimed the other policeman, astonished. "Such a tiny ornament on such a vast surface! You are very lucky, sir." He stooped to retrieve an amulet which he first drew over his lips to obtain its blessing and then handed to Pankh.

It was a miniature Sekhmet, so perfectly carved it seemed the handwork of a god, not of man. Pankh had never owned such a thing, much less dropped it. Its slender chain was woven of tiny gold plackets, but the Sekhmet herself was made of a material he did not at first recognize.

He rubbed the tiny goddess between his thumb and forefinger. It was ivory.

From his palm, the little Sekhmet snarled at him. Under his heavy wig, Pankh's shaved scalp quivered.

Then he remembered he had no patience with religious superstition, and he put the necklace on. "I owe you," he said to the policeman. "I will see that you are well paid for your prompt assistance."

The necklace was surprisingly chilly against his skin. Nor did the heat of his body warm the slender chain. Although the chain was long and did not press up against his throat, he felt strangled by it, and he rubbed his windpipe, straining for air.

"Look there," said the first guard softly. "What are those two doing?"

In the growing light, Pankh made out two people a hundred yards away, admiring the Pyramid. The man, dressed in the ludicrous trousers of northerners, vaulted onto the stone wall that enclosed the Pyramid, built to keep just such people from touching its sacred sides. Little boys had proved particularly annoying in this regard, scrambling over the wall and then with their bare toes trying to find cracks between the Pyramid slabs, so they could crawl upward. They fell and broke bones and their mothers sobbed.

"Tourists even at this hour," said the second guard, shaking his head. "Amazing. And behaving badly, of course, since they're foreigners."

The foreigner stretched out his hand, that he might help his woman up onto the wall with him, and as she was drawing onto her toes, Pankh saw her white gown and long black hair, and recognized the girl of ivory.

*Impossible.*

But true. This foreigner had opened the second shaft. How could a foreigner have known the location? Who could the man be? Some crafty slave, perhaps, or escaped criminal. And what of Renifer? Where was she?

And who had the gold?

For had the girl of ivory still been clothed in gold, he would easily see it from here.

Giving their names to Pankh, so they could be rewarded, the policemen ambled off to deal with the tourists. Pankh had no more time to waste. Slipping around the mastaba, he strode up to the hole. Even in the few minutes that had gone by, there was enough light to see quite well. He descended the long ladder in two steps, crossed the empty treasure room and knelt beside the open trapdoor.

"I will have my gold!" he whispered. "I care for nothing but the gold!"

Pankh stroked the little Sekhmet as if beseeching her.

He forgot that there was one other thing he cared about.

Life.

# STRAT AND ANNIE

The first rays of dawn glinted off Annie's dark hair. Her long white pleated gown lifted gently in the breeze. She seemed ancient and silvery. She could have been a goddess.

"I am starving to death," said Annie dramatically.

He looked at her with great affection. He had saved her from starving to death. Whatever else he had done wrong in his life—and Strat felt assaulted by all he had done wrong in his life—at least he had rescued Annie.

He said, "No one will ever excavate it, because archaeologists care only for kings, but I know where the workmen's village is from here. It takes hundreds of men to do all the stonework, the painting, the road building, the engineering, the cooking. Would a gold sandal be a fair exchange for a jug of water, a loaf of bread and a seat in the shade?"

Annie giggled. "Let's hold out for two jugs of water. Although I would really like an ice cream sundae with chocolate sauce."

He loved her instant recovery. She was not having the vapors, or in need of a rest cure, or weeping on his shoulder, the way girls would in his day. She was bouncing and eager for whatever came next.

He felt a ripping in his soul, as of tendons wrenched from bones because of a fall in a ball game.

What *would* come next?

He sat above her on the wall, Annie standing between his knees staring up at him, thinking his the most beautiful face she had ever seen. Of my precious four days, she thought, more than two are gone. Time is so stingy. "How I missed you," she said, "all these months. But you did the right thing when you saved Katie, Strat, and I have held your noble act in my heart as an example of how to live."

Annie imagined saying those words in 1999 to a boy in her high school. The situation would not come up, though, because boys in her class liked to be examples of how *not* to live. Noble conduct was not a goal in her century.

"Here comes trouble," said Strat softly.

Guards were walking toward them, motioning at Strat to get down. But there was nothing scary about them. They were not armed and dangerous like her tomb escorts. They were just nice guys keeping people off tourist attractions. Annie smiled and waved.

Strat hopped down onto the pavement. "I don't think they know you," he murmured. "They probably weren't part of the sacrifice ritual. They've lost interest now that I'm off their wall. Let's find the workmen's village and buy some food."

Already the cool breezes were gone and the air parched. Huge numbers of people had arrived to take advantage of the short time before the blistering heat began.

Crews were getting to work on funerary chapels and memorial temples. Teams were erecting statues and walling in family cemeteries. Flowers were being delivered, and fine spices and incense being burned. Daughters were visiting their dead mothers and sons paying respect to their ancestors.

Where they had been alone only minutes ago, Annie and Strat were among hundreds now.

"I can hear a choir rehearsing somewhere," she said. "This is so much more fun with you here. I really feel part of ancient Egypt. Of course, I almost *was* part of ancient Egypt. The dead part."

"We are in the center of the City of the Dead," he agreed.

"Thank you," she said, "for keeping me in the city of the living instead," and she began to cry. "Oh, Strat," she whispered, "what should we do about Renifer? She didn't choose the city of the living. Should Renifer have to obey our choice, and not be allowed her choice? Is she still a sacrifice or has she become a suicide?"

Strat looked around him. In the west, where the sands deepened into hills, just before the hills soared into cliffs hundreds of feet high, somewhere tucked among those hills was the workers' village.

"I know," said Annie. "At some point in the day when

nobody's around, we'll go back down and offer her a second chance. I know I'd take it. I'd be sick of dying by then."

Strat took a deep breath. "I think it would be better if we went right now and closed the shaft."

"Strat! You can't mean it!" How had she ever thought that Strat was noble of heart and generous in deed? "That's horrible. Absolutely not! Leaving her there was bad enough. We're not going to be the ones who seal her in!"

"People are going to walk by and find that open hole. They'll explore. They'll find Renifer. She won't be dead because it takes days to starve. Then what? They drag her out? They hand her back to Pharaoh? Will she suffer an even more terrible fate because she circumvented Pharaoh's plan?"

"What could be more terrible than being buried alive?" Annie demanded.

Strat pointed toward the edge of the desert. A hundred yards away, the mutilated corpses of dead men stuck up into the air on tall sharp spikes. Annie had seen that happen; she just hadn't been willing to remember. There was, after all, something worse than running out of air.

"If we close up the shaft, we'll actually be keeping Renifer safe," said Strat. "When it's dark tonight, and everyone else is gone, we pull away the stone and offer her a second chance."

Annie's heartbeat returned to normal. He was a gentleman after all; he had saved Katie; he would save Renifer. It was good.

"Too late," said Strat sadly. "Look. The shaft is already surrounded."

"I can't see," whispered Annie, starting to cry. "What's happening?"

"I don't dare get closer," said Strat. "Quick, up that hill. We can see from there."

They staggered across the sand, which was first hard and flat and then sinking and ankle-breaking, scrabbled up a ragged hillside of sand and climbed rocks that collapsed under their weight. Some places were so steep they were forced to crawl.

"Be careful at the edges," said Strat. "The wind chews on the undersides of these hills, leaving crags supported by nothing."

The crest of the hill was wild and wonderful. Fingers of rock poked out into thin air. The peak of the Pyramid was half a mile away, but eye level. The necropolis stretched on and on. Thousands of distant tomb structures glittered like sugar cubes in the sun.

And where Renifer's open shaft might be, Annie had no idea.

"Let your eye travel down the causeway," said Strat, "and look for a dozen workers with baskets."

"Baskets?" said Annie blankly.

"Rock and sand," said Strat quietly. "That's how they filled in your shaft. Basket after basket. Rock after rock."

And there it was, a team lifting one basket after another from a series of donkey-drawn carts. Somebody somewhere had known about the second shaft.

Strat and Annie clung to each other. They could not, mercifully, hear the sound of the rocks as they dropped down.

But Renifer would.

Annie prayed to her own God that Renifer would not be scared. That she remained proud of her choice. That the end would come quickly for her.

Strat held her until she had stopped weeping.

The sun scorched the desert floor on four sides. He knew that the workmen's village was not far below, but the twists and turns of the jagged hill hid it entirely. Alone, they perched on a rock ledge.

"You're wearing only one sandal," said Strat.

"The other one fell off in the tomb," said Annie. "It's there with Renifer, I guess. I don't know how I managed to keep this one."

Strat took it in his hand. I also held this sandal in another life. Or stole it, depending on who tells the story. He remembered what he had to go back to.

When he set the sandal down, Annie's white dress blew over it, hiding it.

Beyond them, spread out like a painting in five stripes, lay Egypt. Two outside stripes of yellow desert. Narrow green stripes of farmland inside those. The placid brown ribbon of the Nile in the middle. "The river is a sort of vertical oasis, isn't it?" said Annie.

"You are my oasis," said Strat.

He was not sure just how much time he spent telling her that and showing her that. Long enough to know he wanted it to last forever, but long enough to know that time was passing. The heat of noon would be too much on this exposed spot. They must get out of the sun or die under it.

He pulled her even closer, to tell her what he thought they should do next, and Annie screamed.

# PANKH

Pankh was amused.

The foreigners were in each other's arms, oblivious to the world, cooing. He had completely surprised them.

He knew how impressive he looked. Of course, foreigners were always deeply impressed by Egyptians. His white kilt was starched and finely pleated, unlike their sweat-stained garb. His wig was heavy and flawlessly braided, unlike the messy sandy locks of the foreigners. But most important, his dagger was heavy and strong in his hand.

The girl, pleasingly, had screamed.

She would scream more before he was done.

Hetepheres' tomb had been empty. He had spat down the trapdoor, trying to spit on the queen's sarcophagus, but missed.

These were the possibilities: The foreign male had carried the gold in some basket or bundle that Pankh had not seen; or the man had buried it to retrieve later; or somebody else had the gold.

Pen-Meru? Could he have moved so swiftly?

But it was unlikely that Pen-Meru would trust a foreign male. And although Pankh could possibly imagine Pen-Meru saving Renifer, why would anybody save the girl of ivory?

Pankh had climbed out of the tomb, retreated behind the mastaba, dusted himself off and straightened his wig. He was preparing a lie should he encounter the same tomb police when Pharaoh's crew arrived to fill in the shaft.

So Pharaoh had known of the second shaft; known its precise location and that it was empty. But his men had certainly not known that the stone would be moved away and the shaft gaping open, down to where the living sacrifice probably still lived. Pankh laughed grimly to himself as they swore oaths not to tell Pharaoh. His retreat was covered by the racket of rocks they threw down as quickly as they could, to keep the spirit of the sacrifice from reaching out toward their bare feet and cursing their lives.

And there, beyond, were the two foreigners, on the edge of the desert, climbing the cliff. Nobody went toward the desert, where there was no water, no shelter and no hope. People went toward the Nile. Had there been time already to bury the gold up on that cliff? Were they carrying it with them? Or did they expect to meet others with the gold at that spot?

Pankh would get the gold before he threw them off the cliff. No need to worry about bodies. Tomb police didn't bother with this piece of sand. Jackals did.

But now, standing before them, Pankh felt the rage of

frustration working through his chest. They had no gold with them. But they certainly knew where it was; the girl had removed it and placed it somewhere. "Gold," said Pankh clearly. He drew bracelets around his arms and a necklace around his throat and raised his eyebrows.

The foreign boy and girl were puzzled.

"Gold!" he shouted, hating them for not understanding a civilized language. "Where is the gold?"

Their eyes flew open and their jaws dropped. They stared as if seeing somebody rise from the dead.

"The gold," he spat. "Where is the gold?"

"I have the gold," said Renifer, behind him.

Pankh whirled.

Renifer stood on the very edge of the cliff. She was so weighted down with that beautiful gold he did not know how she could possibly have scrambled up here. Behind her was nothing but air.

Pankh recovered quickly. "How beautiful you are, my beloved," he whispered. "How wonderful that you survived Pharaoh's evil trick. How glad I am to see you in the land of the living."

Renifer said nothing. He could not see her breathe or blink. She did not look as if she belonged to the land of the living. Her face was as expressionless as if she had died.

Pankh had his back to the foreign man. He was vulnerable. And yet, he felt in some way that the danger came from Renifer herself. "Come, my beloved. You will hide in my house, lest Pharaoh learn that you survived. But what pleasure we will have in being together, you and I."

Renifer said nothing.

Pankh took a few steps away, hoping Renifer would step toward him. The rims of this kind of cliff frequently caved in, and her weight was putting her in danger. Although of course he could simply retrieve the gold from her corpse. "Renifer, it wasn't my fault. I didn't intend for Pharaoh to sacrifice you. Who could have dreamed that such an idea would enter the mind of a civilized Egyptian? Come to me, my beloved."

Renifer said nothing.

She had not an inch between herself and falling. He extended his hand. But she seemed not to see it. "Your father and I were forced to agree with Pharaoh. My beloved, let us leave these strangers to their own devices. Let us go home and rejoice that you live."

She was still and unearthly in her gold. How *had* she gotten up the steep and difficult slope? Had she been lifted? By what power?

The thin chain of the amulet of Sekhmet seemed to cut his neck.

By now some laborer or priest or guard would have noticed this strange scene playing out on the distant hill. Somebody would investigate. Pankh could not permit Renifer to delay any longer. They would be out of time. "Renifer, come let your beloved Pankh embrace you."

Renifer removed one arm piece. Its gold was over an inch thick. He could not take his eyes off it. Underhanded, she threw the bracelet. The heavy circle sailed in a great arc out beyond the cliff and then vanished in a long curving silent fall.

The sand below was soft. The heavy gold would dig its own hole, the sand would close over it and Pankh would never find it. "No, no, my beloved!" protested Pankh. "You and I will need that gold in our marriage. Think what it will cost to protect you for all time from the wrath of Pharaoh."

Renifer threw a second bracelet into the air.

"Beloved," he said coaxingly, inching toward her.

She almost smiled. She almost softened. She was almost his. When she held out her arms, Pankh acted swiftly, grabbing for those gold-laden wrists, but Renifer leaned back over the cliff edge, planning to fall, still willing to die for Pharaoh.

Pankh's velocity was great. He could not stop himself. Together they would hurtle over the cliff and hundreds of feet down to their deaths. He tried to brace himself against her; let her fall while he saved himself.

But the arm of the foreign male, in its loathsome jacket of heavy cloth, pulled Renifer to safety while Pankh spun out into the air and was lost.

The amulet flew up in Pankh's face, and the last thing he saw before death was the image of Sekhmet, goddess of revenge.

# RENIFER

Renifer stood within the embrace of the foreign male.

She did not need to follow their language to know what they were asking. Fascinated, amazed, they were crying—how did you get here? how did you know? are you all right? we're so glad to see you!

Had the gods sent these strangers to save Renifer—or had she been sent to save them? "I was kneeling beside the sarcophagus while I prayed," she explained, as if they had been given Egyptian along with life. "Pankh looked into the tomb. He did not see me. He had eyes only for gold and thought the tomb empty. He swore, yet again defiling Hetepheres. He damned her for not making her gold available to him. He spat, promising to kill you, O girl of ivory."

The girl had been entrusted to Renifer's care. Handed to Renifer, as it were, in the midst of Pharaoh's papyrus swamp. Renifer could not let Pankh kill the girl of ivory. She had almost literally been on Pankh's heels as he ascended the ladder out of Hetepheres' tomb, too busy muttering to himself and uttering threats to look back. When Pankh hid behind a mastaba, she walked behind a chapel, and then Pharaoh's crew arrived.

For a few moments, she stared at them, as they filled in forever the shaft out of which she had just escaped. She heard their oaths to say nothing to Pharaoh and understood their terror.

Heavy lay the gold on her body. She followed Pankh as he chased the girl of ivory and the foreign male. There was a perfectly fine path up the cliff, but the foreigners and Pankh hadn't seen it, so they struggled up the worst and most crumbling side. Renifer walked slowly along the path. The workers in the village saw her—a goddess, as it were, clothed in gold, going back to her home in the cliffs, and they fell on their faces in the sand and let her pass.

Beyond the Pyramids, the Nile sparkled under the sun. Renifer could see the city of Memphis, her beloved and beautiful home. She could see, from here, the entire world.

And many of its inhabitants, running in her direction.

Pankh had not cried out, but witnesses had. Tourists and guides, vendors of carved wooden hippos or hot spicy sausages—all had shouted to the tomb police that somebody had fallen. A crowd was gathering at the foot of the cliff, exclaiming over Pankh's body. He was an officer of Pharaoh, wearing his uniform. There was no hope of explaining these extraordinary events.

Foreigners would be held responsible.

Nobody would believe any version of Pankh's death except the worst: that he had been pushed to his death by the foreign male. Renifer could see all too clearly what was going to happen now. The boy, who had come to save the girl of ivory and who had just now saved Renifer herself, would be accused of murder, and pay the ultimate price.

The crowd began pointing and shouting, and Renifer knew what they were shouting for. The foreign male.

The girl of ivory turned even more pale, if that were possible, and she and the boy exchanged frightened looks. They had reason to be frightened.

"Go into the desert," said Renifer, pointing at the massive hills in the west. The Nile was truly cupped in a valley, and the sides of the cup were high and brutal. No civilized person went west of the Nile.

"Sekhmet saved me," she said quietly, "and you who protected me will be given protection. Be not afraid. I will prevent the mob from reaching you."

Even now, the boy worried more about Renifer than himself. He wanted her to come too.

She shook her head. "Go, and go swiftly," she said, giving him a gentle push in the right direction.

Coming out of the west, borne on a high wind, was a cloud of sand. It stood up vertically, like an approaching god. The boy and girl walked toward it, while the girl of ivory called farewell, waving, and repeating her accented version of Renifer's name.

How powerful were the gods. Sekhmet had answered every one of Renifer's prayers: Hetepheres' tomb would not be robbed twice, the queen was avenged and Pankh had suffered.

The terror and joy of dying for Pharaoh disappeared. Renifer was astonished and glad to be alive.

She followed the path back down, arriving at the bottom exactly when the soldiers did. They froze at the sight of her.

Renifer extended her long slender arms and stood under the blazing sun, all gold and white, all shimmer and ghost. She sang the chants of the dead, her soprano rising and shivering, curling around the tops of temples as she walked. She flung her head back and addressed the sky and the hidden stars. She called upon Hetepheres to be with her, and Sekhmet to avenge her. She called upon jackals and queens, upon crocodiles and princesses.

Long before she finished her song, the tourists had scurried back to the temples and the guards had fled to the safety of their headquarters. Tomb robbers they would fight. Ghosts and *ka*s would be left to their own devices.

Renifer lowered her arms. They trembled from the weight of the gold.

The tall thin windstorm spread and deepened, until it sailed like a ship over the desert. It flung sand over the half-carved Sphinx, hiding an entire paw. It flung sand over tourists too foolish to shelter in a mausoleum. It smothered the pots of flowers and put out the fires of incense.

Renifer ignored the sand. It would wrap her forever or let her go. She walked on, accepting the will of her gods.

# STRAT

Strat had known they would not die in the tomb of Hetepheres, because when it was uncovered in 1899, it contained no bones. But out here, in the vicious true desert, the one that reached all the way to the Atlantic Ocean, here they could die. No one would know, either. Not in Khufu's time, not in Strat's and not in Annie's.

The footing was terrible.

From a great distance, he had been able to make out tiny paths twisting up those towering cliffs, probably followed by wild goats and greedy robbers. Up close, there were a hundred possible ledges or routes, and no way to tell which actually went somewhere. But in his heart, Strat knew that nothing out here went somewhere. They were headed toward nothing. No town, no oasis, no road, no water.

The sandstorm was no longer a single column. It now covered an entire width of desert. Like a blustery sheet of sand or a hurricane all in a row, its hope was to fill lungs, blind eyes, deafen ears, bury bones.

They came to a bluff, and had to scramble up it, but

their feet sank. They circled it, tripping and stumbling on rocks and rubble. They plunged once more into sand; sand; sand. The wind hurled sand into Annie's eyes, and she cried out, and clung to Strat, wiping at her eyes with her free hand. "It will kill us," she shouted. "We have to go back!"

But they had nothing to go back to. When Strat turned, even the Pyramid of Pharaoh had been obliterated. "Tuck your face beneath my shirt, Annie," he ordered her, "and we will grip each other tightly and hope not to be torn apart by the strength of the wind."

They would be buried where they stood. For a moment he bowed his head over Annie's grit-filled black hair and accepted his defeat. But only for a moment. "No!" he shouted. "I will not be beaten again!"

Strat recognized this shred of his father in him: the refusal to admit defeat. Well, then he had one good thing from Hiram Stratton, Sr., and he would take it.

"Annie," he commanded, "step through Time."

The pain in his heart was so fierce he could not tell whether it was dying of sorrow or of sand. "You go first, Annie. I cannot live a second time in fear that I abandoned you or that you suffered without me. Go. Quickly."

But just as Renifer had refused to leave her tomb, so Annie refused to leave hers. "No, Strat. I love you. Now when Time has finally brought us together, you think I'm leaving? Forget it! Whatever happens, it will happen to both of us."

"Annie, all that can happen to us is death. We have no water, we have no transportation, you don't even have shoes. We cannot live here, only die here. We must cross through Time again."

"But Time won't let us go together and I want to be together. When this storm ends, we'll steal a camel," said Annie. "We'll be our own little wagon train to Morocco. Then we'll build a boat and row across the Atlantic to New York. Although there won't be much around in Manhattan, forty-five hundred years ago." She giggled.

"Stop playing games," said Strat, although this was why he adored her. She could always laugh. Perhaps it was her century; a time when girls seemed to have so much more than the girls in his time. "Anyway, there are no camels in ancient Egypt. If you want to steal a camel, you have to come to 1899 with me."

He expected to hear one of her peculiar words, from the vocabulary of her amazing decade: Okay or Deal.

But Annie's hair swirled across his face in a black cloud, her eyes opened wide, and screaming, she filtered away from him. It was as quick as the death of Pankh. She was in his arms and then his arms were empty.

Strat tried to follow her, stumbling through the sand, falling over rocks, tumbling off the cliff they had so desperately climbed. He felt himself surrounded by all the troops of Pharaoh, reaching and grasping, and then in the sand, he was alone again, retching and gasping. He eluded them, neither dying nor living, just staggering on, calling her name.

*Annie.*

And eventually, he was defeated. Sand filled his shirt and hair, his shoes and the hem of his trousers. His determination not to be beaten had been beaten.

Many things were stronger than one man's heart.

# VII

*The Sands of Time*

# RENIFER

She walked along the edge of the straight-sided canal, wakened a sleeping sailor and ordered him to take her to Memphis. The sandstorm tore his sails and he had to row. Memphis was closed up tight, every shutter and door sealed against the storm. She walked alone through her city.

Sand piled up against the mud-brick walls that enclosed every garden and home. Sand ripped the leaves from the sycamores and tore down the nests of birds. When she reached her own door, she knocked for a long time before the doorkeeper let her in.

Her father, Pen-Meru, was standing in the garden, mournfully surveying the damage from the sandstorm.

Up on the roof, no sand had fallen. On its pedestal still stood the gold statue of Sekhmet. "Greetings, Father, from the *ka* of Hetepheres," said Renifer.

He whirled.

He saw her, goddess and *ka,* cloaked in gold. He who had buried her fell to his knees.

She found it quite pleasing to stand above him. "The

241

queen sent me home. The queen requires you, Father, to treat me as *her* daughter, instead of your own."

Pen-Meru beat his forehead against the dirt and she let this go on for some time. "Enough. The queen requires you to cease stealing. She has, after all, an empty tomb in which to store your living body, should you disobey."

"I obey," whispered Pen-Meru.

Renifer walked into the women's rooms. She would worry about Pharaoh another day. Today she would see her mother, take a hot bath, throw the dreadful gold into a pile by the bed. And maybe she would spend it one day, and maybe she would not. And maybe she would marry one day, and maybe not.

She would not worry. The gods held her in the palm of their hands.

# STRAT

He was buried only up to his ankles, and he shook that sand away, and was aware of raw skin, burning eyes and the terrific heat that rose up to slap him now that the wind had passed. Beyond him stood three Pyramids. One Sphinx. A dozen tents.

Eternity, however desirable, was not here.

Strat was a prisoner of Time. His own.

There was no sign of Annie Lockwood. Instead, he was facing the same group he had left, thousands of years, or only an hour, ago. There stood the girl reporter, his father's hireling, Miss Matthews. How tall she was, her straight spine so unusual. Most females had terrible posture, being desperate to stand lower than their men. The only other girl he knew who was proud of her backbone was Annie herself.

I will never wed, thought Strat. I will never say vows of perpetual love. I will never look for a girl to equal Annie. For there is none.

Dr. Lightner said in an odd voice, "Strat. How can you be holding that gold sandal?"

Strat brushed sand from his eyebrows and hair and

tried to focus on the world in which he was about to be beaten once more. I've just convicted myself, he thought ruefully, staring down at the gold in his hand. I would rather have her lock of hair. This gold sandal is not Annie. And if I learned one thing in the sands of Time, it is that gold has no value. Only decency toward others is to be valued.

"I myself opened the tomb," said Dr. Lightner. "There was but one sandal, Strat, and I hold that in my hand. Where did you find that other one?"

Strat was aware of his father's bulk on his left. The shifting confused figures of the other members of the dig on his right. The flapping of tents and the whisk of brooms, the smack of shovels. There had been a sandstorm. The crew was digging them out.

How could I have let go of Annie, he thought, sunk in misery, and kept my grip on a worthless piece of metal? "It was lying in the rubble," said Strat finally, "up in the hills."

Water was brought, and Strat drank gratefully. Sweet cool water. Now that was treasure.

People spoke of the damage from the sandstorm and of its wondrous works, flinging up from its hidden depths the very partner of the sandal Dr. Lightner had found in a tomb. Strat could not quite hear. The winds of Time spun through his ears and thoughts and made him deaf.

He became aware that his father was speaking, almost courteously. His father seemed to be apologizing. Strat stared at his parent.

"I have judged you wrongly," said Hiram Stratton, Sr. "You are not a thief."

Around them, in this necropolis, more generations of fathers and sons were on display than anywhere on earth. Here had a thousand generations loved and hated. And what was Strat's destiny? To love or to hate?

"I wish you to come home with me," said Hiram Stratton, Sr., "and be my son."

"You said that once before, Father," said Strat softly. "When you snatched me from school and put me in an insane asylum."

"I was wrong," said his father.

Neither Strat nor any other person had ever heard those words from the mouth of Hiram Stratton, Sr. Strat was touched beyond measure that his father would make such an effort, such an admission. Could it be? he thought. Could my father and I be at peace? Could that be the gift of Time?

Not Annie, but my father? My family? Those I want so badly to love and cannot?

# CAMILLA

Camilla Matthews was looking at Hiram Stratton, Sr. She was looking at evil.

Good people, because they are good, want to believe in good. She saw Strat wanting to believe that his father was good. Leaning into the hope that his father cared for him after all. Would welcome him home. Would love him.

How the world was driven by love. This was a desperate love; a son's love.

Hiram Stratton was gloating, revenge within his reach. Camilla understood because she, too, was a friend of revenge. This was a man who excelled at cheating and pretending and convincing all around him to believe his untruths.

Camilla said softly, "Strat, there is a place for you in the British war. Go south. Vanish again. Use a different name. Carry on in a different life." She took his hand and turned him and gave him a slight shove toward the south.

Far away, as if somebody at that very moment were painting her on a gold background, Camilla could almost make out a shadowy girl in a white gown. "Go, Strat," said Camilla softly and insistently. "Go, and I will give you time."

Strat stared into Camilla's eyes. *"You were sent by Time?"*

"Go," she said, and he went.

Hiram Stratton, Sr., opened his huge maw to bellow after his son.

Camilla caught the sleeve of the man's jacket. He weighed far more than she, but she was taller and her touch startled him, and he paused.

"It is not your son, at this moment, who matters, Mr. Stratton."

The great man looked at her with annoyance and shook himself loose.

"I am the daughter of Michael Mateusz, whose death you gladly caused when you burned your factory. I stand here, Hiram Stratton, to accuse you of murder."

# STRAT

Strat ran after Annie. "We'll go to the Sudan!" he shouted over the sand. "The British are having a wonderful war! I'll get another camera. We'll sell your gold sandal and have enough to live on for a while. We'll sail up the Nile and catch the army and I'll be a famous photographer! Annie! Wait!"

He struggled on and on in the sand. He could not seem to reach her. He told himself he would catch up. "We'll get married," he said. "It would be unseemly to travel together otherwise. I know that I am but nineteen, Annie, and I have no means of properly supporting you. But I have faith in my wits and my abilities!"

He was exhausted. His voice did not carry the way he wanted it to. He was not getting closer to her. "Be my wife, Annie! We shall find a missionary on the banks of the Nile! Or in South Africa! Or on board some fine ship!"

He and Annie would repeat their vows in the presence of God and this company, whoever the company might be. Strat was not picky. He had known the worst of companies. Annie was always eager for adventure. She was no shrinking violet, like the girls in his time.

But like a violet, Annie shrank. He could see her and he could not.

His voice—or perhaps it was hers—cried out, "It isn't fair!"

He lunged forward, sure he could take her hand. But Annie whirled like some dervish of ancient Egypt, spinning and diminishing and vanishing. No! thought Strat. We're going to honeymoon in a far land and make a home as homes are meant to be: children and hope and joy and love.

He could see the Nile in the distance, a dark and shining ribbon, like the ribbons of Annie's hair, and he ran on and on, sure he could reach them both.

# ANNIE

"No!" screamed Annie Lockwood. "It isn't fair! I came all the way through Time for you, Strat, and you—"

Her voice had no sound and her lungs no air. She wanted to beat her fists upon the chest of Time. This isn't fair! You brought me all this way! I deserve Strat!

How many times had Annie or her classmates shouted that? It isn't fair! In nursery school, when other kids got pushed on the swings and your turn never came. In third grade, when other kids got to sit next to their best friend, but you had to sit with a creep. In sixth, when other kids got to go to Disneyland for vacation, but you just grilled hotdogs in the backyard. In ninth grade, when you paid some attention to the world, and found that some citizens were treated a lot better than other citizens.

It isn't fair!

But by then, enough things had not been fair that you could shrug. Life isn't fair, you said to one another. But this is me, thought Annie. I should be an exception.

Time, like all the great powers, like gravity or velocity, continued on. It did not acknowledge what happened inside or outside its span. Annie fell, hair in her face, all sweat and tangles, desperate for a drink of water. The thirst of the desert had taken all moisture out of her. She could not open her eyes in the tremendous glare.

Slowly the rushing shriek of wind and Time left her ears. She tried to listen to the sounds around her, to separate speech from noise, but she was too battered by Time and loss. She tried to see where she was, but the immensity of sun blinded her, and she could make out only stones and mirages of water and palm. She wavered in her heart, as if she were nothing but heat on sand, a figment, impossible to catch up to, impossible to be.

It didn't really matter where or when Annie was, because she was not quite where or when. She was among but had not arrived.

She knew that Egypt did not care. Egypt had seen too much. From Alexander the Great consulting the oracle out in the western sands to the invasion by Napoleon. From Antony romancing Cleopatra on the deck of a Roman ship to the canal at Suez. From the ancient scribe who chiseled a decree of Ptolemy V on a slab of black basalt to Champollion who translated the Rosetta Stone, two thousand years later.

I don't care one little twitch about history! thought Annie. I want Strat. It isn't fair.

She had never felt quite so American or quite so spoiled brat, but she did not want to set an example. At last she stood up and stumbled over stones and steps toward a drinking fountain. The water was cold and refreshing and she drank as if she had not had a sip of water in a thousand years. She felt as if she had not showered in a thousand years either. She tottered back to the seat she had left.

*I love you. I want to marry you. We'll have children and joy and hope and love.*

Had she said that? Or had Strat? Or were the words a dream?

*I love you. I want to marry you. We'll have children and joy and hope and love.* Couldn't have been me saying that, thought Annie dully. In my time, the most a girl ever says is, "You wanna go to a movie?" and the most a boy ever says is, "Yeah, okay, if I got nothin' else to do."

"The museum is closing," said a bored voice.

Annie looked up, jarred. For a moment, she almost recognized the man; his ancient dark features; somebody's father, somebody's murderer—he was—no. He was only a guard, sweeping through the museum at closing. And she, Annie, was only a tourist, not even a New Yorker.

She was just a silly girl in silly clothing, wearing silly hopes.

"Oh, Strat," she said, heart bursting with grief.

And across the room—not a room, really, but a vast, glass-ceilinged case; a case large enough to hold an entire ancient temple and an entire reflecting pool and three entire classes of middle school children on a field trip—across that room, somebody heard.

"Annie?" said Strat.

# CAMILLA

The unfounded accusations of a girl had no effect.

Hiram Stratton, Sr., merely explained who and what she was, a paid lackey of his own, a piece of chicanery whose ticket he had paid for.

The silly and very rude words of Miss Matthews embarrassed the company. The French were appalled, as always, by the manners of American females. The Germans were amused by so dramatic a woman, built to sing opera, to stand by the Rhine and bellow songs across the water.

Hiram Stratton, Sr., shoved the girl aside and demanded of all of them—servant and scholar, expert and passerby, "Find my son. Now."

The Americans returned to the dig and the tourists got bored. The Egyptians melted away and the British remembered that they were en route to war.

Camilla went to her tent to pack. What would become of her now? Her dream of becoming a great reporter had been silly to start with, but now she had proved herself a liar and a fake, and nobody needed a reporter with those vices. Her tears soaked into the clothing she was folding.

She had not avenged her father.

She had not done anything, really.

She no longer knew what she had been thinking of—telling Strat to run off into the desert. It was true that great heat caused a lady to hallucinate.

Well, she could do one thing: sail to Spain and talk to Katie, who knew right from wrong, action from apathy and hope from sorrow.

"Miss Matthews?" called Dr. Lightner through the flimsy tent walls. "Might we speak?"

She wiped away her tears. Men were undone by ladies' weeping and that was not fair. Oh, the scorn Dr. Lightner would face, having been tricked by a mere girl. "Of course, sir. Please come in. I am packing. I shall not abuse your hospitality another hour."

He entered, stooping of course, because neither he nor she could stand upright in the tents. He pulled up a stool and sat beside her. "You should have told me. I would not have exchanged a syllable with the man had I known that he truly is a beast and a murderer."

"You believe me?"

"Of course I believe you. You have not forgotten the life and death of your father, nor should you. How proud your father would be, Miss Matthews. Such courage! To become a famous reporter and cross half the world!"

She faced him squarely. "But you know that isn't true. I am not Camilla Matthews, age thirty and a seasoned reporter. I am Camilla Mateusz and I am seventeen." She lifted her chin and told him every detail, those he had heard already in front of witnesses and those she had lacked the courage to state.

When she finished the true narrative of her life, he was staring aghast. She awaited his contempt. But no, he was shouting with laughter. Kissing her!

"Forgive me," he said. "I was forward. I deeply apologize. But oh, Miss Matthews! I thought you a queen all along. In my thoughts, I compared you to the queens of ancient Egypt. Partly, that was your fine height and straight spine, your carriage and manner. Although of course," he corrected himself, "the real queens of ancient Egypt, whose mummies I myself have examined, were short and bent. Yet I was correct. You are as royalty. What zest! What courage! Camilla, how proud I am that you trust me with the truth."

She had to laugh. "I have no royal blood, sir. I am the daughter of Polish immigrants. And I have no idea what is to become of me except that I must leave."

"Leave? Do not think of such a thing! Might I have the honor of asking you to become Camilla Lightner?" he said. His words tumbled over one another in his excitement. "We will live in Cairo. I will support your family. I promise, no matter how badly I need donations, to accept none from Hiram Stratton. If necessary, I will become a professor of history in some obscure American college attended by dull and unworthy students. I will do anything to support you properly and not compromise your high standards."

He was a good man.

Was it possible that she could be a good woman?

She thought of Katie, and thought she could hear Katie laughing, saying, of course you can. Goodness is a decision. Make it now.

"Yes," said Camilla.

"What children we will have!" cried Archibald Lightner, kissing her once more. "How brave and strong they will be!"

"And tall," said Camilla.

# ANNIE

The person coming toward her ... was he the boy from lunch? Or could it possibly be Strat from another century? He looked like Strat and he didn't. He wore cargo pants and a navy sweater. Strat in Egypt had worn khaki trousers with frayed hems, red socks inside scratched old boots.

The boy worked his way through a crowd of departing kids, dodging their swinging backpacks. "Here you are!" he said, laughing. "I've been looking and looking for you. I don't know how we got separated. Did you finish the special exhibition without me?"

"Hurry it up, kids," said the guard. "Take a left out that door, please."

They took a left out that door and walked like strangers away from the Egyptian Room. So, Time, what are you up to? Annie wanted to know. Flinging me from century to century? Giving me an hour here and a minute there? And who is this? And why isn't his identity clear?

"I'm taking a train home," she said to the boy. "I'm walking to the station. It's a long way on foot, but a

257

beautiful part of the city." She framed her next sentence the way Strat would have. "Might I have the pleasure of your company?"

"I love how you said that. Now I feel like an usher at a wedding." He put out his arm for her to take. They walked down an aisle strewn with sculpture instead of wedding guests. "This has been the weirdest day," he confided. "I was trying to find you, since I didn't want to lose my new Lockwood on the very day we met, and I guess I dozed off in the Egyptian Room. I dreamed I was on the Nile, sailing upstream with a bunch of British soldiers. We didn't have enough to eat and the tribes were attacking from both banks and what I did have was a camera. On a tripod, isn't that a kick? I lost it in a swamp. There was a crocodile."

Annie was trembling. She swallowed hard and asked the important thing. "Was there a girl with you? Did she catch up? Did you have company?"

But he was frowning at his watch, lifting his wrist and tapping on the watch face. "It isn't working," he said, completely distracted by not knowing the time.

I don't know Time very well, either, thought Annie. "Don't worry about the watch," she told him. "All it is is Time. We're going to have enough."

He smiled at her. "I love how you said that, too. I love people who are sure of things." He took the watch off and squinted at it to see what was wrong.

Then they were outdoors, the wide magnificent museum steps stretching down to the street. "Two at a time," he told her, and in the lamplit night, they vaulted down the wide steps two at a time until they reached the sidewalk below.

It was a beautiful evening. The air was crisp but not cold. New York glittered with early Christmas lights and hundreds of people moved swiftly to their unknown destinations. The whole world seemed eager to get home in time.

The boy balled up his watch and aimed for a trash barrel.

"Don't throw your watch out," cried Annie.

"It's a really cheap one. I shouldn't have expected it to last. You can't get this kind of watch fixed, you can only get another."

"May I keep it for a souvenir?" said Annie quickly, and blushed at his stare. "After all, I don't meet extra Lockwoods all the time."

He laughed and gave her the watch. "I've noticed," he said as they walked, "that just about every sentence we've said has the word time in it." He said, "Are you warm enough without gloves?" He took her hand in his. "Listen," he said, "speaking of time, what are you doing next Saturday?"

Who cares about other times and other worlds when you can dream about next weekend? thought Annie. The best time is always now. "I'm free," said Annie Lockwood to Lockwood Stratton.

She put the broken watch on her own wrist because she had seen right away why the watch didn't work.

It was full of sand.

# FACTS

The Metropolitan Museum of Art did have an exhibition in November 1999 presenting the tomb artifacts of Hetepheres, mother of Khufu, who built the Great Pyramid. It was a mysterious tomb. Her sarcophagus, although sealed in antiquity, contained no mummy. The tomb, small as a closet, contained much less than a queen should have. George Reisner, who excavated that tomb in real life in 1925, guessed that it was a hurried reburial, possibly after a botched robbery.

The tomb entrance was found during the Reisner dig when the cameraman's tripod broke some plaster.

That did not happen, however, in 1899, and the cameraman was not Strat.

No Hiram Stratton, Sr., or Hiram Stratton, Jr., existed or made donations to the museum.

# ABOUT THE AUTHOR

Caroline B. Cooney is the author of many young adult novels. They include *The Ransom of Mercy Carter; Tune In Anytime; Burning Up; The Face on the Milk Carton* (an IRA-CBC Children's Choice Book) and its companions, *Whatever Happened to Janie?* (an ALA Best Book for Young Adults), *The Voice on the Radio* and *What Janie Found; What Child Is This?* (an ALA Best Book for Young Adults); *Driver's Ed* (an ALA Best Book for Young Adults and a *Booklist* Editors' Choice); *Among Friends; Twenty Pageants Later;* and the first three books in the Time Travel Quartet, *Both Sides of Time, Out of Time* and *Prisoner of Time*. Caroline B. Cooney lives in Westbrook, Connecticut.